Jommy Cross was only nine when the secret police shot his mother. His father had been killed already, and Jommy had to find a way to survive in a hostile world until he reached the full powers of Slan maturity. 'Granny' offered him one – living in a hovel and keeping alive by stealing, using his telepathic powers to avoid detection, gleaning knowledge from every intelligent mind that passed his way . . . Jommy had to prepare himself for the day when his father's science could liberate humans and Slans from the blinding hatred which made them destroy each other. But were there any other Slans left? And were the gruesome stories humans told of Slan atrocities true? Jommy had to find out . . .

Also by A. E. van Vogt in Panther Books

Destination : Universe !
The War against the Rull
The Voyage of the Space Beagle
The Book of Ptath
Moonbeast
Away and Beyond

A. E. van Vogt

Slan

Panther

Granada Publishing Limited
Published in 1960 by Panther Books Ltd
Frogmore, St Albans, Herts AL2 2NF
Reprinted 1968, 1970, 1974, 1975

First published in Great Britain by
Weidenfeld & Nicolson Ltd 1953
Made and printed in Great Britain by
Hunt Barnard Printing Ltd
Aylesbury, Bucks
Set in Monotype Plantin

To my wife
E. Mayne Hull

1

HIS MOTHER'S HAND felt cold, clutching his.

Her fear as they walked hurriedly along the street was a quiet, swift pulsation that throbbed from her mind to his. A hundred other thoughts beat against his mind, from the crowds that swarmed by on either side, and from inside the buildings they passed. But only his mother's thoughts were clear and coherent —and afraid.

"They're following us, Jommy," her brain telegraphed. "They're not sure, but they suspect. We've risked once too often coming into the capital, though I did hope that this time I could show you the old slan way of getting into the catacombs, where your father's secret is hidden. Jommy, if the worst happens, you know what to do. We've practised it often enough. And, Jommy, don't be afraid, don't get excited. You may be only nine years old, but you're as intelligent as any fifteen-year-old human being."

Don't be afraid. Easy to advise, Jommy thought, and hid the thought from her. She wouldn't like that concealment, that distorting shield between them. But there were thoughts that had to be kept back. She mustn't know he was afraid also.

It was new and exciting, as well. He felt excited each time he came into the heart of Centropolis from the quiet suburb where they lived. The great parks, the miles of skyscrapers, the tumult of the throngs always seemed even more wonderful than his imagination had pictured them—but then size was to be expected of the capital of the world. Here was the seat of the government. Here, somewhere, lived Kier Gray, absolute dictator of the entire planet. Long ago—hundreds of years before—the slans had held Centropolis during their brief period of ascendancy.

"Jommy, do you feel their hostility? Can you sense things over a distance yet?"

He strained. The steady wave of vagueness that washed from the crowds pressing all around grew into a swirl of mind clamour. From somewhere came the stray wisp of thought:

"They say there are still slans alive in this city, in spite of all precautions. And the order is to shoot them on sight."

"But isn't that dangerous?" came a second thought, obviously a question asked aloud, though Jommy caught only the mental picture. "I mean a perfectly innocent person might be killed by mistake."

"That's why they seldom shoot on sight. They try to capture them and then examine them. Their internal organs are different from ours, you know, and on their heads are—"

"Jommy, can you feel them, about a block behind us? In a big car! Waiting for reinforcements to close in on us from in front. They're working fast. Can you catch their thoughts, Jommy?"

He couldn't! No matter how hard he reached out with his mind and strained and perspired with his trying. That was where her mature powers surpassed his precocious instincts. She could span distances and disentangle remote vibrations into coherent pictures.

He wanted to turn around and look, but he didn't dare. His small, though long, legs twinkled underneath him, half running to keep up with his mother's impatient pace. It was terrible to be little and helpless and young and inexperienced, when their life demanded the strength of maturity, the alertness of slan adulthood.

His mother's thoughts stabbed through his reflections: "There are some ahead of us now, Jommy, and others coming across the street. You'll have to go, darling. Don't forget what I've told you. You live for one thing only: to make it possible for slans to live normal lives. I think you'll have to kill our great enemy, Kier Gray, even if it means going to the grand palace after him. Remember, there'll be shouting and confusion, but keep your head. Good luck, Jommy."

Not until she had released his hand, after one quick squeeze, did Jommy realize that the tenor of her thoughts had changed. The fear was gone. A soothing tranquillity flowed from her brain, quieting his jumping nerves, slowing the pounding of his two hearts.

As Jommy slipped into the shelter made by a man and a woman walking past them, he had a glimpse of men bearing down on the tall figure of his mother, looking very ordinary and very human in her slacks and pink blouse, and with her hair caught up in a tightly knotted scarf. The men, dressed in civilian clothes, were crossing the street, their faces dark with an expression of an unpleasant duty that had to be done. The thought of that unpleasantness, the hatred that went with it, was a shadow in their minds that leaped out at Jommy. It puzzled him even in this moment when he was concentrating on escape. Why was it necessary that he should die? He and this wonderful, sensitive, intelligent mother of his! It was all terribly wrong.

A car, glittering like a long jewel in the sun, flashed up to the curb. A man's harsh voice called loudly after Jommy: "Stop! There's the kid. Don't let that kid get away! Stop that boy!"

People paused and stared. He felt the bewildering mildness of their thoughts. And then he had rounded the corner and was racing along Capital Avenue. A car was pulling away from the curb. His feet pattered with mad speed. His abnormally strong fingers caught at the rear bumper. He pulled himself aboard and hung on as the car swung into the maze of traffic and began to gather speed. From somewhere behind came the thought:

"Good luck, Jommy."

For nine years she had schooled him for this moment, but something caught in his throat as he replied: "Good luck, Mother."

The car went too fast, the miles reeled off too swiftly. Too many people paused in the street and stared at the little boy clinging so precariously to the shining bumper. Jommy felt the intensity of their gazes, the thoughts that whipped into their minds and brought jerky, shrill shouts to their lips. Shouts to a driver who didn't hear.

Mists of thought followed him then, of people who ran into public booths and telephoned the police about a boy caught on a bumper. Jommy squirmed, and his eyes waited for a patrol car to swing in behind and flag the speeding auto to a halt. Alarmed, he concentrated his mind for the first time on the car's occupants.

Two brain vibrations poured out at him. As he caught those thoughts, Jommy shuddered, and half lowered himself toward the pavement, prepared to let go. He looked down, then dizzily pulled himself back into place. The pavement was a sickening blur, distorted by the car's speed.

Reluctantly, his mind fumbled into contact again with the brains of the men in the car. The thoughts of the driver were concentrated on his task of manoeuvring the machine. The man thought once, flashingly, of a gun carried in a shoulder holster. His name was Sam Enders, and he was the chauffeur and body-guard of the man beside him—John Petty, chief of the secret police of the all-powerful Kier Gray.

The police chief's identity penetrated through Jommy like an electric shock. The notorious slan hunter sat relaxed, indifferent to the speed of the car, his mind geared to a slow, meditative mood.

Extraordinary mind! Impossible to read anything in it but a blur of surface pulsations. It wasn't, Jommy thought, amazed, as if John Petty could be consciously guarding his thoughts. But there was a shield here as effective in hiding true thoughts as any slan's. Yet it was different. Overtones came through that told of a remorseless character, a highly trained and brilliant brain. Suddenly there was the tail end of a thought, brought to the surface by a flurry of passion that shattered the man's calm: "—I've got to kill that slan girl, Kathleen Layton. That's the only way to undermine Kier Gray—"

Frantically, Jommy attempted to follow the thought, but it was gone into the shadows, out of reach. And yet he had the gist.

7

A slan girl named Kathleen Layton was to be killed so that Kier Gray might be undermined.

"Boss," came Sam Enders' thought, "will you turn that switch? The red light that flashed on is the general alarm."

John Petty's mind remained indifferent. "Let them alarm," he snapped. "That stuff is for the sheep."

"Might as well see what it is," Sam Enders said.

The car slackened infinitesimally as he reached to the far end of the switchboard; and Jommy, who had worked his way precariously to one end of the bumper, waited desperately for a chance to leap clear. His eyes, peering ahead over the fender, saw only the long, bleak line of pavement, unrelieved by grass boulevards, hard and forbidding. To leap would be to smash himself against concrete. As he drew back hopelessly, a storm of Enders' thoughts came to him as Enders' brain received the message on the general alarm:

"—all cars on Capital Avenue and vicinity watch for boy who is believed to be a slan named Jommy Cross, son of Patricia Cross. Mrs. Cross was killed ten minutes ago at the corner of Main and Capital. The boy leaped to the bumper of a car, which drove away rapidly, witnesses report."

"Listen to that, boss," Sam Enders said. "We're on Capital Avenue. We'd better stop and help in the search. There's ten thousand dollars' reward for slans."

Brakes screeched. The car decelerated with a speed that crushed Jommy hard against the rear end. He tore himself free of the intense pressure and, just before the car stopped, lowered himself to the pavement. His feet jerked him into a run. He darted past an old woman, who clutched at him, avarice in her mind. And then he was on a vacant lot, beyond which towered a long series of blackened brick and concrete buildings, the beginning of the wholesale and factory district.

A thought leaped after him from the car, viciously: "Enders, do you realize that we left Capital and Main ten minutes ago? That boy—There he is! Shoot him, you fool!"

The sense of the man Enders drawing his gun came so vividly to Jommy that he felt the rasp of metal on leather in his brain. Almost he saw the man take aim, so clear was the mental impression that bridged the hundred and fifty feet between them.

Jommy ducked sideways as the gun went off with a dull *plop*. He had the faintest awareness of a blow, and then he had scrambled up some steps into an open doorway, into a great, dark-lit warehouse. Dim thoughts reached out from behind him:

"Don't worry, boss, we'll wear that little shrimp out."

"You fool, no human being can tire a slan." He seemed to be barking orders then into a radio: "We've got to surround the

8

district at 57th Street. . . . Concentrate every police car and get the soldiers out to—"

How blurred everything was becoming! Jommy stumbled through a dim world, conscious only that, in spite of his tireless muscles, a man could run at least twice as fast as his best speed would carry him. The vast warehouse was a dull light-world of looming box shapes, and floors that stretched into the remote semidarkness. Twice the tranquil thoughts of men moving boxes somewhere to his left impinged on his mind. But there was no awareness of his presence in their minds, no knowledge of the uproar outside. Far ahead, and to his right, he saw a bright opening, a door. He bore in that direction. He reached the door, amazed at his weariness. Something damp and sticky was clinging to his side, and his muscles felt stiff. His mind felt slow and unwieldy. He paused and peered out of the door.

He was staring into a street vastly different from Capital Avenue. It was a dingy street of cracked pavement, the opposite side lined with houses that had been built of plastic a hundred or more years before. Made of virtually unbreakable materials, their imperishable colours basically as fresh and bright as on the day of construction, they nevertheless showed the marks of time. Dust and soot had fastened leechlike upon the glistening stuff. Lawns were ill-tended, and piles of debris lay around.

The street was apparently deserted. A vague whisper of thought crept forth from the dingy buildings. He was too tired to make certain the thoughts came only from the buildings.

Jommy lowered himself over the edge of the warehouse platform and dropped to the hard concrete of the street below. Anguish engulfed his side, and his body had no yield in it, none of the normal spring that would have made such a jump easy to take. The blow of striking the walk was a jar that vibrated his bones.

The world was darker as he raced across the street. He shook his head to clear his vision, but it was no use. He could only scamper on with leaden feet between a gleaming but sooty two-storey house and a towering, streamlined, sea-blue apartment block. He didn't see the woman on the veranda above him, or sense her, until she struck at him with a mop. The mop missed because he caught its shadow just in time to duck.

"Ten thousand dollars!" she screamed after him. "The radio said ten thousand. And it's mine, do you hear? Don't nobody touch him. He's mine. I saw him first."

He realized dimly that she was shouting at other women who were pouring out of the tenement. Thank God, the men were at work!

The horror of the rapacious minds snatched after him as he fled with frightened strength along the narrow walk beside the apartment building. He shrank from the hideous thoughts and flinched from the most horrible sound in the world: the shrill voice clamour of people desperately poor, swarming in their dozens after wealth beyond the dreams of greed.

A fear came that he would be smashed by mops and hoes and brooms and rakes, his head beaten, his bones crushed, flesh mashed. Swaying, he rounded the rear corner of the tenement. The muttering mob was still behind him. He felt their nervousness in the turgid thoughts that streamed from them. They had heard stories about slans that suddenly almost overshadowed the desire to possess ten thousand dollars. But the mob presence gave courage to individuals. The mob pressed on.

He emerged into a tiny back yard piled high with empty boxes on one side. The pile reared above him, a dark mass, blurred even in the dazzle of the sun. An idea flashed into his dulled mind, and in an instant he was climbing the piled boxes.

The pain of the effort was like teeth clamped into his side. He ran precariously along over the boxes, and then half lowered himself, half fell into a space between two old crates. The space opened all the way to the ground. In the almost darkness his eyes made out a deeper darkness in the plastic wall of the tenement. He put out his hands and fumbled around the edges of a hole in the otherwise smooth wall.

In a moment he had squeezed through and was lying exhausted on the damp earth inside. Pieces of rock pressed into his body, but for the moment he was too weary to do anything but lie there, scarcely breathing, while the mob raged outside in frantic search.

The darkness was soothing, like his mother's thoughts just before she told him to leave her. Somebody climbed some stairs just above him, and that told him where he was: in a little space underneath back stairs. He wondered how the hard plastic had ever been shattered.

Lying there, cold with fear, he thought of his mother—dead now, the radio had said. Dead! She wouldn't have been afraid, of course. He knew only too well that she had longed for the day when she could join her dead husband in the peace of the grave. "But I've got to bring you up, Jommy. It would be so easy, so pleasant, to surrender life; but I've got to keep you alive until you're out of your childhood. Your father and I have spent what we had of life working on his great invention, and it will have been all for nothing if you are not here to carry on."

He pushed the thought from him, because his throat suddenly ached from thinking of it. His mind was not so blurred now. The brief rest must have helped him. But that made the rocks on which he lay more annoying, harder to bear. He tried to shift his body, but the space was too narrow.

Automatically, one hand fumbled down to them, and he made a discovery. They were shards of plastic, not rocks. Plastic that had fallen inward when the little section of the wall had been smashed and the hole through which he had crawled was made. It was odd to be thinking of that hole and to realize that somebody else—*somebody out there*—was thinking of the same hole. The shock of that blurred outside thought was like a flame that scorched through Jommy.

Appalled, he fought to isolate the thought and the mind that held it. But there were too many other minds all around, too much excitement. Soldiers and police swarmed in the alleyway, searching every house, every block, every building. Once, above that confusion of mind static, he caught the clear, cold thought of John Petty:

"You say he was last seen right here?"

"He turned the corner," a woman said, "and then he was gone!"

With shaking fingers Jommy began to pry the pieces of shard out of the damp ground. He forced his nerves to steadiness, and began with careful speed to fill the hole, using damp earth to cement the pieces of plastic. The job, he knew with sick certainty, would never stand close scrutiny.

And all the time he worked he felt the thought of that other person out there, a sly, knowing thought, hopelessly mingled with the wild current of thoughts that beat on his brain. Not once did that somebody else stop thinking about this very hole. Jommy couldn't tell whether it was a man or woman. But it was there, like an evil vibration from a warped brain.

The thought was still there, dim and menacing, as men pulled the boxes half to one side and peered down between them—and then, slowly, it retreated into distance as the shouts faded and the nightmare of thoughts receded farther afield. The hunters hunted elsewhere. For a long time Jommy could hear them, but finally life grew calmer, and he knew that night was falling.

Somehow the excitement of the day remained in the atmosphere. A whisper of thoughts crept out of the houses and from the tenement flats, people thinking, discussing what had happened.

At last he dared wait no longer. Somewhere out there was the mind that had *known* he was in the hole and had said nothing. It was an evil mind, which filled him with unholy premonition, and urgency to be away from this place. With fumbling yet swift fingers, he removed the plastic shards. Then, stiff from his long vigil, he squeezed cautiously outside. His side twinged from the movement, and a surge of weakness blurred his mind, but he dared not hold back. Slowly he pulled himself to the top of the boxes. His legs were lowering to the ground when he heard rapid footfalls—and the first sense of the person who had been waiting there struck into him.

A thin hand grabbed his ankle, and an old woman's voice said triumphantly: "That's right, come down to Granny. Granny'll take care of you, she will. Granny's smart. She knew all the time you could only have crept into that hole, and those fools never suspected. Oh, yes, Granny's smart. She went away, and then she came back and, because slans can read thoughts, she kept her mind very still, thinking only of cooking. And it fooled you, didn't it? She knew it would. Granny'll look after you. Granny hates the police, too."

With a gasp of dismay, Jommy recognized the mind of the rapacious old woman who had clutched at him as he ran from John Petty's car. That one fleeting glimpse had impressed the evil old one on his brain. And now, so much of horror breathed from her, so hideous were her intentions, that he gave a little squeal and kicked out at her.

The heavy stick in her free hand came down on his head even as he realized for the first time that she had such a weapon. The blow was mind-wrecking. His muscles jerked in spasmodic frenzy. His body slumped to the ground.

He felt his hands being tied, and then he was half lifted, half dragged for several feet. Finally he was hoisted on to a rickety old wagon, and covered with clothes that smelled of horse sweat, oil and garbage cans.

The wagon moved over the rough pavement of the back alley, and above the rattling of the wheels Jommy caught the old woman's snarl. "What a fool Granny would have been to let them catch you. Ten thousand reward— Bah! I'd never have gotten a cent. Granny knows the world. Once she was a famous actress, now she's a junk woman. They'd never give a hundred dollars, let alone a hundred hundred, to an old rag and bone picker. Bah on the whole lot! Granny'll show them what can be done with a young slan. Granny'll make a huge fortune from the little devil—"

2

THERE WAS that nasty little boy again.

Kathleen Layton stiffened defensively, then relaxed. There was no escape from him where she stood at the five-hundred-foot battlements of the palace. But it should be easy, after these long years as the only slan among so many hostile beings, to face anything, even Davy Dinsmore, age eleven.

She wouldn't turn. She wouldn't give him any intimation that she knew he was coming along the broad, glass-enclosed promenade. Rigidly, she held her mind away from his, maintaining the barest contact necessary to keep him from coming upon her by surprise. She must keep right on looking at the city, as if he weren't there.

The city sprawled in the near distance before her, a vast reach of houses and buildings, their countless colorations queerly shadowed now and subdued, seemingly dead in the gathering twilight. Beyond, the green plain looked dark, and the normally blue, gushing water of the river that wound out of the city seemed blacker, shiningless, in that almost sunless world. Even the mountains on the remote, dimming horizon had taken on a sombre hue, a grim moodiness that matched the melancholy in her own soul.

"Ya-a-ah! You better take a good look. It's your last."

The discordant voice rasped on her nerves like so much senseless noise. For a moment, so strong was the suggestion of completely unintelligible sounds, the meaning of the words did not penetrate to her consciousness. And then, in spite of herself, she jerked around to face him.

"My last! What do you mean?"

Instantly, she regretted her action. Davy Dinsmore stood there less than half a dozen feet away. He had on long green silken trousers, and a yellow shirt open at the neck. His little boy's face with its "I'm-a-tough-guy" expression, and his lips twisted into a sneer, reminded her forcibly that even noticing him was a victory for him. And yet—what could have made him say a thing like that? It was hard to believe that he'd have thought of such words himself. The brief impulse to investigate further in his mind seized her. She shuddered, and decided against it. Entering that brain in its present state would sicken her outlook for a month.

It was a long time, months and months, since she had cut

herself off from mental contact with the stream of human thoughts, human hopes and human hates that made a hell of the palace atmosphere. Better to scorn the boy now, as she had in the past. She turned her back on him, and her slightest of slight connections with his brain brought her the overtones of the rage that surged through him at the action. And then there was his jangling voice again:

"Ya-a-ah, the last time! I said it, and I mean it. Tomorrow's your eleventh birthday, isn't it?"

Kathleen made no answer, pretending she hadn't heard. But a sense of disaster pierced her unconcern. There was too much gloating in his voice, too much certainty. Was it possible that dreadful things had been going on, dreadful plans made, during these months that she had kept her mind insulated from the thoughts of these people? Was it possible she had made a mistake in locking herself away in a world of her own? And now the real world had smashed through her protective armour?

Davy Dinsmore snapped: "Think you're smart, don't you? Well, you won't feel so smart when they're killing you tomorrow. Maybe you don't know it yet, but Mamma says the word is going around the palace now that when they first brought you here, Mr. Kier Gray had to promise the cabinet that he'd have you killed on your eleventh birthday. And don't think they won't do it, either. They killed a slan woman in the street the other day. That shows! What do you think of that, smarty?"

"You're—crazy!" The words were forced from her lips. She hardly realized she had uttered them, because they weren't what she thought. Somehow, she did not doubt that he spoke the truth. It fitted in with their mass hatred. It was so logical that she seemed, suddenly, always to have known it.

Oddly enough, it was the mention of his mother having told Davy that held Kathleen's mind. It took her memory back three years to a day when this boy had attacked her under the benevolent eyes of his mother, thinking to bully a small girl. What a surprise, what a screaming and kicking with fear there had been as she held him aloft, until his outraged parent had rushed forward, uttering threats of what she was going to do to "a dirty, sneaking little slan."

And then, suddenly, there had been Kier Gray, grim and tall and powerful, and Mrs. Dinsmore cringing before him.

"Madam, I wouldn't lay a hand on that child if I were you. Kathleen Layton is a property of the State, and in due course the State will dispose of her. As for your son, I happened to observe the entire proceedings. He got exactly what every bully deserves, and I hope he has learned his lesson."

How she had thrilled at his defence of her! And after that she had put Kier Gray in a different category in her mind from that occupied by other human beings, in spite of his ruthlessness, in spite of the terrible stories about him. But now she knew the truth, and that he had meant no more than he said: ". . . the State will dispose of her."

With a start, she emerged from her bitter reverie and saw that in the city below a change had taken place. The whole great mass had donned its nighttime splendour with a billion lights twinkling in far-flung panorama. Wonder city now, it spread before her, a vast, sparkling jewel, an incredible fairyland of buildings that reared grandly toward the heavens and blazed a dream picture of refulgent magnificence. How she had always longed to go into that mysterious city and see for herself all the delights her imagination had built up. Now, of course, she would never see it. An entire world of glory would remain unseen, untasted, unenjoyed.

"Ya-a-ah!" came Davy's discordant voice again. "Take a good look. It's the last time."

Kathleen shivered. She couldn't stand the presence of this . . . this wretched boy another second. Without a word, she turned and went down into the palace, down to the loneliness of her bedroom.

Sleep would not come, and it was late. Kathleen knew it was late, because the clamour of outside thoughts had dimmed, and people were long gone to bed, except for the guards, the nervous, and party-goers.

Funny she couldn't sleep. Actually, she felt easier, now that she knew. The day-to-day life had been horrible, the hatred of the servants and most of the other human beings an almost unbearable strain. She must have dozed finally, for the harsh thought that came to her from outside did twisting things to the unreal dream she was having.

Kathleen stirred restlessly. The slan tendrils (thin strands like burnished gold glinting dully in the semi-light against the dark hair that crowned her finely moulded, childish face) lifted clear of her hair and waved gently, as if a soft breeze had caught them. Gently yet insistently.

Abruptly, the menacing thought those sensitive antennae drew out of the night-enveloped palace of Kier Gray penetrated. Kathleen awakened, quivering.

The thought lingered in her mind for an instant, distinct, cruel, cold-bloodedly murderous, shocking the sleep from her like a douche of ice water. And then it was gone, as completely as if it had never existed. There remained only a dim confusion of mind pictures that washed in a never-ending stream from the countless rooms of the vast palace.

Kathleen lay very still, and from the depths of her own mind there came the realization of what this meant. Somebody was not waiting until tomorrow. Somebody doubted that her execution would take place. And he intended to present the council with an accomplished fact. There could be only one such person, powerful enough to face any consequences: John Petty, the head of the secret police, the fanatic antislan—John Petty, who hated her with a violence that, even in this den of antislans, was dismaying. The assassin must be one of his henchmen.

With an effort, she quieted her nerves and strained her mind out, to the limit of her powers. The seconds dragged, and still she lay there groping, searching for the brain whose thoughts had for a brief flash threatened her life. The whisper of outside thoughts became a roar that shook her brain. It was months since she had explored that world of uncontrolled minds. She had thought the memory of its horrors had not dimmed. Yet the reality was worse than the memory. Grimly, with an almost mature persistence, she held herself in that storm of mind vibration, fighting to isolate each individual pattern in turn. A sentence came:

"Oh, God, I hope they don't find out he's cheating. Today, on the vegetables!"

That would be the wife of the assistant chef, wretched God-fearing woman, who lived in mortal terror of the day when the petty thievery of her husband would be discovered.

Briefly, Kathleen felt sympathy for the tortured little woman lying awake beside her husband there in the darkness. But not too much sympathy, for that little woman had once, on sheer, vicious impulse, paused as Kathleen was passing her in a corridor and without preliminary mental warning slapped her hard in the face.

Kathleen's mind pressed on, driven now by a mounting sense of urgency. Other pictures flitted through her brain, a veritable kaleidoscope, brushed aside almost at the moment of entry as unwanted, unrelated to the menace that had awakened her. There was the whole world of the palace with its intrigues, its countless personal tragedies, its hard ambitiousness. Dreams with psychological implications were there, from people who tossed in their sleep. And there were pictures of men who sat scheming far into the night.

Abruptly, then, it came, a wisp of crude purpose, the hard determination to kill *her*! Instantly, it was gone again, like an elusive butterfly, only not like that at all. The deadliness of it was like a spur that rowelled her to desperation. For that second flash of menacing thought had been too powerful for it to be anything but near, terribly, dangerously near.

Amazing how hard it was to find him again. Her brain ached, her body felt cold and hot by turns; and then a stray picture came for a third time—and she had him. And now she understood why his brain had evaded her so long. His thoughts were so carefully diffused, deliberately flashing to a thousand different subjects, seeming simply overtones to the confusion of mind noises all around.

He must have practised it, but even so, he wasn't a John Petty or a Kier Gray, either of whom could hold rigidly to a line of reasoning without once slipping up. Her would-be assailant, in spite of all his cleverness, had given himself away. As soon as he entered the room she would—

The thought broke off. Her mind soared toward disintegration with the shock of the truth that showered in upon her. The man was inside her bedroom, and was at this very instant creeping on his knees toward her bed.

A sense of time suspension came to Kathleen as she lay there. It grew out of the darkness, and the way the blankets held her down, covering even her arms. There was the knowledge that the slightest move would rustle the stiff sheets. He'd rush her then before she could move, pin her down under the blankets and have her at his mercy.

She couldn't move. She couldn't see. She could only feel the gathering excitement that pulsed through the mind of the killer. His thoughts were quicker, and he had forgotten to diffuse them. The flame of his murderous purpose was a burning thing within him, so fierce and powerful that she had to turn part of her mind away, because it was suddenly like a physical hurt.

And in that full revelation of this thought, Kathleen read the story of the attack. This man was the guard who had been posted outside her door. But it wasn't the usual guard. Odd she hadn't noticed the change. They must have been switched while she slept. Or else she had been too upset by her own thoughts.

She caught his plan of action as he rose up on the carpeted floor and bent over the bed. For the first time her eyes caught the dim flash of the knife as his hand drew back for the plunge.

Only one thing to do. Only one thing she *could* do! With a swift, firm heave, she flung the blankets up over the head and shoulders of the startled man. Then she was sliding out of the bed—a shadow among the shadows of the room.

Behind her, the man uttered a faint cry as the blankets, flung by her small, extraordinarily strong arms, enveloped him. There was dismay in that low yell, and the first fear of what discovery would mean.

She caught his thoughts, heard his movements as he leaped the bed in a single jump and began flailing out with his arms, searching the dark reaches of the room. Queerly, then it seemed to her that she shouldn't have left the bed. If death were to come tomorrow anyway, why delay it? But she knew the answer in the surging will to live that swept her; and in the thought, for the second time, that this midnight visitor was proof that someone who wanted her dead feared there would be no execution.

She drew a deep breath. Her own excitement was submerging in the first formulation of contempt for the clumsy efforts of the assassin. "You fool," she said, her child's voice hot with disdain, yet immensely unchildlike in its stinging logic, "do you actually believe that you can catch a slan in the darkness?"

It was pitiful the way the man leaped in the direction from which her words came and beat with his fists in every direction. Pitiful and horrible because his thoughts were ugly now with terror. There was something unclean in such fear that made Kathleen shiver where she stood in her bare feet at the opposite side of the room.

Once more she spoke in her high, childish voice: "You'd better leave before somebody hears you stumbling around. I won't report you to Mr. Gray if you leave right away."

The man didn't believe her, she saw. There was too much fear in him, too much suspicion and, suddenly, cunning! With a muttered curse he stopped searching for her, and flung himself recklessly toward the door, where the light switch was located. She felt him draw a gun as he groped for the switch. And realized that he preferred to take the chance of attempting to escape the guards who would come running at the sound of a gunshot, to meeting his superior with a confession of failure.

"You silly fool!" said Kathleen.

She knew what she must do, in spite of never having done it before. Soundlessly she slid along the wall, fingers searching. Then she had opened a panelled door, slipped through it, locked it behind her and raced along a dim-lit private corridor to a door at the end. It opened at her touch onto a large, luxuriously furnished office room.

In sudden fright at the boldness of her action, Kathleen stood in the doorway, staring at the powerful-looking man who sat at a desk writing by the light of a shaded desk lamp. Kier Gray did not look up immediately. She knew after a moment that he was aware of her presence and she took courage from his silence to observe him.

There was something magnificent about this ruler of men that held her admiration even now, when the fear of him lay like a weight inside her. The strong features of the man formed a noble countenance, now thoughtfully bent over the letter he was writing.

As he wrote, she was able to follow the surface of his thought, but nothing else. For Kier Gray, she had found out long ago, shared with that most hateful of men, John Petty, the ability to think in her presence without deviation, in a manner that made

18

mind reading a practical impossibility. Only those surface thoughts were there, the words of the letter he was writing. And her excitement and impatience overrode any interest in his letter. She burst out, "There's a man in my room. He tried to kill me."

Kier Gray looked up. His face held a harder expression now that it was turned full upon her. The noble qualities of the profile were lost in the determination and power of that lean, strong jaw. Kier Gray, master of men, stared at her coldly. When he spoke, his mind moved with such precision, and voice and mind were so closely co-ordinated, that she wasn't sure whether or not he had actually uttered any words.

"An assassin, eh? Go on."

The story poured from Kathleen's lips in a trembling stream of words that covered everything that had happened from the time Davy Dinsmore had mocked at her on the battlements.

"So you think John Petty is behind it?" he asked.

"He's the only one who could have done it. The secret police control the men who guard me."

He nodded slowly, and she sensed the faintest tension in his mind. Yet his thoughts were deep and calm and slow. "So it's come," he said softly. "John Petty's bid for supreme power. I almost feel sorry for the man, he is so blind to his own short-comings. No chief of secret police has ever held the confidence of a people. I am worshipped and feared; he is only feared. And he thinks that all-important."

Kier Gray's brown eyes looked gravely into Kathleen's. "He intended to kill you in advance of the date fixed by the council because I could do nothing about it once it was done. And my helplessness to act against him, he knew, would lower my prestige with the council." His voice was very low now, as if he had forgotten Kathleen's presence and was thinking out loud. "And he was right. The council would only be impatient if I tried to force an issue over the death of a slan. And yet, they would take no action as proof that I was afraid. Which would mean the beginning of the end. Disintegration, a splitting into groups growing gradually more hostile to each other as the so-called realists sized up the situation and picked the probable winner, or started that pleasant game known as playing both ends against the middle."

He was silent for a moment, then he continued: "As you can see, Kathleen, a very subtle and dangerous situation. For John Petty, in order to discredit me with the council, has been very assiduous in spreading the story that I meant to keep you alive. Accordingly, and this is the point that will interest you"—for the first time a smile broke over the bleak lines of Kier Gray's face—

"accordingly, my prestige and position now depend upon my ability to keep you alive in spite of John Petty."

He smiled again. "Well, what do you think of our political situation?"

Kathleen's nostrils dilated with contempt. "He's a fool to go against you, that's what I think. And I'll help you all I can. I *can* help, with reading minds and things."

Kier Gray smiled a broad smile that lighted up his whole countenance and erased the harsh lines from his face. He said, "You know, Kathleen, we human beings must seem very queer at times to slans. For instance, the way we treat you. You know the reason for that, don't you?"

Kathleen shook her head. "No, Mr. Gray. I've read people's minds about it, and nobody seems to know why they hate us. There's something about a war between slans and human beings long ago, but there were wars before that, and the people didn't hate each other afterward. And then there are all those horrible stories too absurd to be anything but dreadful lies."

He said, "You've heard what slans do to human babies?"

"It's one of the silly lies," Kathleen said contemptuously. "They're all dreadful lies."

He chuckled. "I can see you have heard about it. And this may shock you: such things do happen to babies. What do you know about the mental outlook of an adult slan, whose intelligence is two to three hundred per cent higher than that of a normal human being? All you know is that you wouldn't do such things, but you're only a child. Anyway, never mind that now. You and I are in a fight for our lives. The assassin has probably escaped from your room by now, but you have to look into his mind to identify him. We'll have our showdown now. I'll get Petty here, and the council. They won't like being awakened from their beauty sleep, but to hell with them! You stay here. I want you to read their minds and tell me afterward what they thought during the investigation."

He pressed a button on his desk and said curtly into a little boxlike instrument: "Tell the captain of my personal guard to come to my office."

3

IT WASN'T EASY to sit under the dazzling lights that had been turned on. The men looked at her too often, their thoughts a mixture of impatience and mercilessness, and no pity for her anywhere. Their hatred weighed upon her spirit, and dimmed the life that throbbed along her nerves. They hated her. They wanted her dead. Appalled, Kathleen closed her eyes and turned her mind away, and tried to flatten herself back into her chair as if by sheer will power she might make her body invisible.

But there was so much at stake, she dared not miss a single thought or picture. Her eyes and mind jerked open, and there it was again—the room, the men, the whole menacing situation.

John Petty stood up abruptly and said, "I object to the presence of this slan at this meeting on the grounds that her innocent, childlike appearance might influence some of us to be merciful."

Kathleen stared at him wonderingly. The chief of the secret police was a heavily built man of medium height, and his face, which was rather corvine than aquiline, and the slightest degree too fleshy, showed not a trace of kindliness. Kathleen thought: Did he really believe *that*? Any one of these people merciful, for any reason!

She tried to read behind his words, but his mind was blurred deliberately, his dark, powerful face expressionless. She caught the faintest overtone of irony, and realized that John Petty understood the situation perfectly. This was his bid for power; and his whole body and brain were alert and deadly with the tremendousness of the knowledge.

Kier Gray laughed dryly and suddenly Kathleen caught the glow of the man's magnetic personality. There was a tigerish quality about the leader, immensely fascinating, a flamelike aura that made him alive as was no one else in the room. He said, "I don't think we have to worry about . . . about our kindly impulses overpowering our common sense."

"Quite right!" said Mardue, minister of transport. "A judge has to sit in the presence of the accused." He stopped there, but his mind carried the sentence on: "—especially if the judge knows in advance that the judgment is death." He chuckled softly to himself, his eyes cold.

"Then I want her out," snarled John Petty, "because she's

a slan, and by heaven, I won't have a slan sitting in the same room with me!"

The answering surge of collective emotion to that popular appeal struck Kathleen like a physical blow. Voices rose up, raging:

"You're damned right!"

"Put her out!"

"Gray, you've got an almighty nerve waking us up in the middle of the night like this—"

"The council settled all this eleven years ago. I didn't even know about it until recently."

"The sentence was death, was it not?"

The hail of voices brought a grim smile to Petty's lips. He glanced at Kier Gray. The two men's eyes crossed like rapiers preliminary to a deadly thrust. It was easy for Kathleen to see that Petty was trying to confuse the issue. But if the leader felt himself losing, it was not visible in his impassive face; nor did a ripple of doubt flicker into his mind.

"Gentlemen, you are under a misapprehension. Kathleen Layton, the slan, is not on trial here. She is here to give evidence against John Petty, and I can well understand his desire to have her out of the room."

John Petty's amazement then was a little overdone, Kathleen analyzed. His mind remained too calm, too icily alert, as his voice took on a bull-like roar.

"Well, of all the damned nerve! You've awakened all of us out of our sleep to pull a two-o'clock-in-the-morning surprise trial on me—on the evidence of a slan! I say you've got an almighty nerve, Gray. And, once for all, I think we should settle right now the juridical problem of whether a slan's word can be taken as evidence of any kind."

There it was again, the appeal to basic hatreds. Kathleen shivered before the waves of answering emotion that swept out from the other men. There was no chance for her here, no hope, nothing but certain death.

Kier Gray's voice was almost stolid as he said, "Petty, I think you should know that you're not talking now to a bunch of peasants whose minds have been roused by propaganda. Your listeners are realists, and, in spite of your obvious attempts to befuddle the issue, they realize that their own political and perhaps physical lives are at stake in this crisis which you, not I, have forced upon us."

His face hardened into a thin bleak line of tensed muscles. His voice took on a harsh rasp. "I hope that everyone present will wake up from whatever degree of sleep, emotionalism or impatience controls him to realize this: John Petty is making this bid to depose me, and no matter who wins between us, some of you are going to be dead before morning."

They weren't looking at her now. In that suddenly still room, Kathleen had the sensation of being present but no longer visible. It was as if a weight had been removed from her mind, and she could see and feel and think for the first time with normal clarity.

The silence in that fine oak-panelled room was mental as well as sonal. For a moment the thoughts of the men were blurred, diminished in intensity. It was as if a barrier had been flung up between her mind and theirs, for their brains worked on deep, deep inside them, exploring, gauging chances, analysing the situation, tensing against a suddenly realized, deadly danger.

Kathleen grew abruptly aware of a break in the blur of thoughts, a clear, sharp, mental command to her: "Go to the chair in the corner, where they can't see you without twisting their heads. Quick!"

Kathleen flung one glance at Kier Gray. She saw his eyes almost glaring at her, so fierce was the blaze in them. And then she slipped off her chair without a sound, obeying him.

The men didn't miss her, weren't even aware of her action. And Kathleen was conscious of a glow as she realized that Kier Gray, even in this moment of strain, was playing his cards without missing a trick. He spoke aloud:

"Of course, there is no absolute necessity for executions, provided John Petty once and for all gets out of his head this insane desire to replace me."

It was impossible now to read the thoughts of the men as they stared speculatively at Kier Gray. For the moment each man was intent; briefly, all their minds were as controlled as were John Petty's and Kier Gray's, their whole consciousness concentrated on what they *should* say and *should* do.

Kier Gray went on, the faintest tinge of passion in his voice: "I say insane because, though it may seem that this is simply a squabble for power between two men, it is more than that. The man who has supreme power represents stability and order. The man who wants it must, the moment he attains power, secure himself in his position. This means executions, exiles, confiscations, imprisonment, torture—all, of course, applied against those who have opposed him or whom he distrusts.

"The former leader cannot simply step down into a subordinate role. His prestige never actually vanishes—as witness Napoleon and Stalin—therefore he remains a permanent danger. But a would-be leader can simply be disciplined and put back on his job. And that is my plan for John Petty."

He was, Kathleen saw, appealing to their cautious instincts, their fear of what change would involve. Her thoughts broke off as John Petty sprang to his feet. For a moment he was off guard, but so great was his rage that it was as impossible to read his thoughts as if he were in full control of his mind.

"I think," he burst out, "I have never heard such an extraordinary statement from a presumably sane man. He has accused me of befuddling the issue. Gentlemen, have you realized that he has as yet produced no issue, no evidence? All we have are his statements, and the dramatic trial which he has sprung on us in the middle of the night, when he knew that most of us would be drugged with sleep. I must confess that I'm not fully awake, but I am, I think, awake enough to realize that Kier Gray has succumbed to that gnawing disease of dictators of all ages, the persecution complex. I have no doubt that for some time past he has read into our every word and action some threat against his position.

"I can hardly find words to express my dismay at the thought of what this means. With the slan situation so desperate, how could he even suggest that one of us would precipitate disunion? I tell you, sirs, we cannot afford even the hint of a split at the present time. The public is on edge over the monstrous world-wide activity of the slans against human babies. Their attempt to slanize the human race, with its resultant horrible failures, is the greatest problem that has ever confronted a government."

He turned to Kier Gray, and Kathleen felt a chill at the perfection of his acting, his apparent sincerity. "Kier, I wish that I could forget what you have done. First, this trial, then the threat that some of us will be dead before morning. Under the circumstances, I can only suggest that you resign. You no longer have my confidence, at least."

Kier Gray said with a thin smile, "You see, gentlemen, we now come to the core of the problem. He wants my resignation."

A tall, thin, youngish man with a hawklike face spoke up harshly. "I agree with Petty. Your actions, Gray, have shown that you are no longer a responsible person. Resign!"

"Resign!" cried another voice, and suddenly it sounded like a bedlam chorus: "Resign! Resign! Resign!"

To Kathleen, who had been following John Petty's words with concentrated attention, the words and the harsh accompanying thoughts sounded like the end. A long moment passed before she realized that four of the seated ten had done all the shouting.

Her mind straightened painfully. So that was it. By crying "Resign!" over and over, they had hoped to stampede the doubtful and the fearful and, for the time being, had failed. Her mind and her eyes flashed toward Kier Gray, whose very presence had kept the others from yielding to panic. Just looking at him brought a return of courage. For there he sat, a little straighter in his chair, now looking taller, bigger, stronger; and on his face was an ironical, confident smile.

24

"Isn't it odd," he asked quietly, "how the four younger men rally to the support of young Mr. Petty? I hope that it is obvious to the older gentlemen present that here is advance organization, and also that there will be firing squads before morning because these young firebrands are transparently impatient of us old fogies—for, in spite of my being in their age level, they do regard me as an old fogy. They're wild to throw off the restraint we have exercised, and are, of course, convinced that by shooting the oldsters they will only hasten by a few years what nature would, in any event, manage to do in the course of time."

"Shoot 'em!" snarled Mardue, the oldest man present.

"The damned young upstarts!" snapped Harlihan, airways minister.

There was a muttering among the older men that would have been good to hear if Kathleen hadn't been so acutely aware of the impulses behind the words. Hatred was there, and fear, and doubt and arrogance, frustration and determination—all were there, a tangle of mental squalor.

The faintest bit pale, John Petty faced that muttering. But Kier Gray leaped to his feet, eyes blazing, fists clenched: "Sit down, you unutterable fool! How dared you precipitate this crisis now, when we may have to change our entire slan policy? We're losing, do you hear? We haven't got a scientist to match the superscientists of the slans. What wouldn't I give to have one of them on our side! To have, say, a slan like Peter Cross, who was stupidly murdered three years ago because the police who caught him were tainted by the mentality of the mob.

"Yes, I said 'mob'. That's all people are these days. A mob, a beast we've helped build up with our propaganda. They're afraid, mortally afraid for their babies, and we haven't got a scientist who can think objectively on the matter. In fact, we haven't got a scientist worthy of the name. What incentive is there for a human being to spend a lifetime in research when in his mind is the deadening knowledge that all the discoveries he can hope to make have long since been perfected by the slans? That they're waiting out there somewhere in secret caves, or written out on paper, ready for the day when the slans make their next attempt to take over the world?

"Our science is a joke, our education a mass of lies. And every year the wreck of human aspirations and human hopes piles higher around us. Every year there's greater dislocation, more poverty, more misery. Nothing is left to us but hatred, and hatred isn't enough. We've either got to terminate the slans or make terms with them and end this madness."

Kier Gray's face was dark with the passion he had put into his words. And all the time, Kathleen saw, his mind was calm, watchful, cautious. Master of demagoguery, ruler of men, when he spoke again his voice seemed flat in comparison, his magnificent baritone clear and soft.

"John Petty has accused me of wanting to keep this child alive. I want you all to think back over the past few months. Has Petty at any time ever remarked to you, laughingly perhaps, that I intended to keep her alive? I know that he has, because it came to my ears. But you see what he's been doing, subtly spreading the poison. Your political minds will tell you that he has forced me into this position: by killing her, I will seem to have yielded, and thereby will lose prestige.

"Therefore I intend to issue a statement saying that Kathleen Layton will not be executed. In view of our lack of knowledge of slans, she will be kept alive as a study subject. I, personally, am determined to make the best of her continued presence by observing the development of a slan to maturity. I have already made a tremendous body of notes on the subject."

John Petty was still on his feet. "Don't try to shout me down!" he snarled. "You've gone too far. Next thing you'll be handing over a continent to the slans on which they can develop these so-called superinventions of which we have heard so much but never seen. As for Kathleen Layton, by heaven, you will keep her alive over my dead body. The slan women are the most dangerous of all. They're the breeders, and they know their job, damn them!"

The words blurred for Kathleen. Into her mind, for the second time, had come an insistent question from Kier Gray: "How many present are for me unconditionally? Use your fingers to indicate."

One startled look she sent him, and then her mind skewered into the welter of emotions and thoughts that flooded from the men. It was hard, for there were many thoughts, there was much interference. And besides, her brain began to weaken as she saw the truth. Somehow, she had believed the older men were all for the leader. And they weren't. In their minds was fear, a growing conviction that Kier Gray's days were numbered, and they had better play along with the young, strong group.

At last, dismayed, she held three fingers up. Three out of ten in favour, four definitely against him and with Petty, three wavering.

She couldn't give him those last two figures because his mind didn't ask for anything more. His attention was concentrated on her three fingers, his eyes the faintest bit wide and alarmed. For the barest moment it seemed to her that anxiety flickered through his thoughts. And then the impassivity closed over his mind and countenance. He sat in his chair, like a figure of stone, cold and grim and deadly.

She couldn't take her eyes off the leader.

The conviction came that here was a cornered man, racking his brain, searching back into his experience for a technique to turn the imminent defeat into victory. She struggled to penetrate that brain, but his iron grip on his thoughts, the very lucid, straightforward motion of his mind, remained an unshakable barrier between them.

But in those surface thoughts she read his doubts, a queer uncertainty that yet held within it no fear, simply hesitation as to what he should do, *could* do, next. That seemed to mean that he had not really foreseen a crisis of such proportions, an organized opposition, a smouldering hatred of himself awaiting only the opportunity to overthrow and destroy him. Her thought ended as John Petty said:

"I think we ought to take a vote on this matter now."

Kier Gray began to laugh, a long, deep, cynical laugh that ended on a note of surprisingly good humour. "So you'd like to vote on an issue that a moment ago you said I hadn't even proved to be existent! Naturally I refuse to appeal to the reason of those present any longer. The time for reason has passed when deaf ears are turned, but just for the sake of the record, a demand for a vote at this time is an implicit admission of guilt become openly arrogant, the result, no doubt, of the security engendered by the support of at least five, possibly more, of the council. Let me put one more of my cards on the table. I have known of this rebellion for some time and have prepared for it."

"Bah!" said Petty. "You're bluffing. I've watched your every move. When we first organized this council we feared eventualities such as one man dispensing with the votes of the others, and the safeguards then set up are still in force. Each of us has a private army. My own guards are out there, patrolling the corridor, and so are the guards of every member of the council, ready to rush at each other's throats when the word is given. We are quite prepared to give it and take our chance of being killed in the battle that results."

"Ah," said Kier Gray softly, "now we're out in the open."

There was a shuffling of feet among the men, a chilling spray of thoughts; and then, to Kathleen's dismay, Mardue, one of the three she had thought in unconditional support of Kier Gray, cleared his throat. She caught the thought of his weakening resolve just before he spoke.

"Really, Kier, you're making a mistake in regarding yourself as dictator. You're only elected by the council, and we have a perfect right to elect someone in your place. Someone, perhaps, who will be more successful in organizing the extermination of the slans."

It was turncoating with a vengeance. The rats were deserting the sinking ship and trying desperately now, Kathleen saw, to convince the new powers that their support was valuable.

In Harlihan's brain, too, the wind of thought was blowing in a new direction. "Yes, yes. Your talk about making a deal with the slans is treason—pure treason. That's the one untouchable subject so far as the mo . . . the people are concerned. We must do something to exterminate the slans, and perhaps a more aggressive policy on the part of a more aggressive man—"

Kier Gray smiled wryly; and still that uncertainty was in his brain—what to do, what to do? There was a vague suggestion of something else, a tensing to the situation, a darkening resolution to take a chance. But nothing tangible, nothing clear, came to Kathleen.

"So," Kier Gray said, still in his soft voice, "you would turn the chairmanship of this council over to a man who, only a few days ago, allowed Jommy Cross, nine years old, probably the most dangerous slan alive today, to escape in his own car."

"At least," said John Petty, "there's one slan who won't escape." He stared malevolently at Kathleen, then turned triumphantly toward the others. "Here's what we can do—execute her tomorrow; in fact, right now, and issue a statement that Kier Gray was removed from office because he had come to a secret agreement with the slans, and his refusal to kill Kathleen Layton was proof of it."

It was the strangest thing in the world to be sitting there, listening to that death sentence and feeling no emotion, as if it weren't herself they were talking about. Her mind seemed far away, detached, and the murmur of agreement that rose up from the men also had that odd distortion of distance.

The smile faded from Kier Gray's face. "Kathleen," he said aloud sharply, "we might as well stop playing. How many are against me?"

She stared at him blurrily and heard herself replying tearfully: "They're all against you. They've always hated you because you're so much smarter than they are, and because they think you've kept them down and overshadowed them, and made it seem as if they're not important."

"So he uses her to spy on us," John Petty snarled, but there was triumph in his rage. "Well, at least it's pleasant to know that we're all agreed on one thing—that Kier Gray is through."

"Not at all," said Kier Gray mildly. "I disagree so violently that all eleven of you will face firing squads within ten minutes. I was undecided about taking such drastic action, but now there is no alternative and no going back because I have just taken an irrevocable action. I have pressed a button advising the eleven officers in command of your guard, your most trusted advisers, *and your heirs*, that the hour has come."

They stared at him stupidly as he went on:

"You see, gentlemen, you failed to allow for a fateful flaw in human nature. The desire of underlings for power is as great as your own. The solution to such a situation as came up today was suggested to me some time ago when Mr. Petty's chief aide approached me with the offer that he would always be willing to replace Mr. Petty. I made it a policy then to explore the matter further, with very satisfying results, and saw to it that the men were on the scene for Kathleen's eleventh birth—ah, here are the new councillors!"

The door burst open and eleven grim young men with drawn revolvers came in. There was a great shout from John Petty: "Your guns!" And a wailing cry from one man: "I didn't bring one!" And then the crash of revolver shots filled the room with an echoing, re-echoing roar.

Men writhed on the floor, choking in their own blood. Through a blur, Kathleen saw one of the eleven councillors still standing, smoking gun in hand. She recognized John Petty. He had fired first. The man who had thought to replace him was dead, a motionless figure on the floor. The chief of the secret police held his gun steady, pointed at Kier Gray, as he said, "I'll kill you before they can get me unless you make a deal. I'll co-operate, naturally, now that you've turned the tables so neatly."

The leader of the officers glanced inquiringly at Kier Gray. "Shall we let him have it, sir?" he asked. He was a lean, dark man with an aquiline face and a sharp baritone voice. Kathleen had seen him around the palace occasionally. His name was Jem Lorry. She had never tried to read his mind before, but now she realized that he also had a power of control over his thoughts that defied penetration. However, there was enough of his character on the surface of his mind to show him for what he was: a tough, calculating and ambitious man.

"No," Kier Gray replied thoughtfully. "John Petty will be useful. He'll have to agree that the other men were executed as a result of the investigations of his police disclosing secret arrangements with the slans.

"That will be the explanation—it always works on the poor, bewildered mass of fools outside. We owe the idea to Mr. Petty himself, but I think we were capable of thinking of it ourselves. However, his influence will be valuable in putting it over. In fact," he said cynically, "I believe the best method is to give Petty credit for the executions. That is, he was so horrified at his discovery of their perfidy, he acted on his own initiative, and then threw himself on my mercy, which, in view of the serious evidence he produced, I naturally granted at once. How's that?"

Jem Lorry came forward. "Good stuff, sir, And now there's one thing I'd like to make clear, and I speak for all of the new councillors. We need you, your terrific reputation, your brains, and we're willing to help make you a god to the people—in other words, to help consolidate your position and make it unassailable —but don't think you can make arrangements with our chief officers to kill *us*. *That* won't work again."

Kier Gray said coldly, "It's hardly necessary to tell me anything so obvious. Clear this carrion out, and then—we've got some planning to do. As for you, Kathleen, go to bed. You're in the way now."

As she hurried off, shaking now from reaction, Kathleen wondered: In the way? Did he just mean— Or did he mean— After the murders she had witnessed, she couldn't be sure of him, of anything. It was a long, long time before sleep came.

4

FOR JOMMY CROSS there were long spells of darkness and mental blankness that merged finally into a steely grey light through which vague thoughts at last wove a web of reality. He opened his eyes, conscious of great weakness.

He was lying in a little room, staring up at a smeared, dirty ceiling, from which some of the plaster had fallen. The walls were an uneven grey, splotched with age. The pane of the single window was cracked and discoloured; the light that forced its way through fell across the end of the iron bedstead in a little pool and lay there as if exhausted from the effort.

Its wan brightness revealed bedclothes that were remnants of what had once been grey blankets. At one edge, straw stuck out from the old mattress, and the whole thing stank with a stale, unaired odour. Sick though he still was, Jommy flung the foul coverings from him and started to slip out of bed. A chain rattled menacingly, and there was sudden pain in his right ankle. He lay back, panting from the exertion, and stunned. He was chained to this loathsome bed!

Heavy footsteps aroused him from the stupor into which he had fallen. He opened his eyes to see a tall, gaunt woman in a formless grey dress standing at the door, her black eyes gleaming down at him like bright beads.

"Ah," she said. "Granny's new boarder has come out of his fever, and now we can get acquainted. That's good! That's good!"

She rubbed her dry hands together raspingly. "We're going to get along beautifully, aren't we? But you've got to earn your keep. No slackers can leech off Granny. No, sir. We'll have to have a heart-to-heart talk about that. Yes, yes," she leered at him over clasped hands, "a heart-to-heart talk."

Jommy stared up at the old woman in repelled fascination. As the thin, slightly stooped creature sank with a grunt onto the foot of the bed, he drew his legs up against his body, withdrawing as far from her as the chain would allow. It struck him that he had never seen a face that more nearly expressed the malignant character that lay behind the mask of old flesh. With rising disgust, he compared her thin, lined, egg-shaped head with the mind inside; and it was all there. Every twisted line in that wrecked face had its counterpart in the twisted brain. A whole world of lechery dwelt within the confines of that shrewd mind.

His thought must have shown in his face, for she said with sudden savagery, "Yes, yes, to look at Granny you'd never think she was once a famous beauty. You'd never suspect that men once worshipped the white loveliness of her. But don't forget that this old hag saved your life. Never forget that, or Granny may turn your ungrateful hide to the police. And how they'd love to have you. How they would love it! But Granny's kind to them that's kind to her and does as she wants."

Granny! Was there ever a term of affection more prostituted than by this old woman calling herself Granny!

He searched her mind, trying to find in its depths her real name. But there was only a blur of pictures of a silly, stage-struck girl, profligate of her charms, ruined, degraded to the level of the street, hardened and destroyed by adversity. Her identity was buried in a cesspool of the evil she had done and thought. There was an endless story of thieving. There was the dark kaleidoscope of more loathsome crimes. There was murder committed—

Shuddering, immeasurably weary now that the first stimulus of her presence was fading, Jommy withdrew from the abomination that was Granny's mind. The old wretch leaned toward him, her eyes like gimlets drilling into his.

"It's true," she asked, "that slans can read minds?"

"Yes," Jommy admitted, "and I can see what you're thinking, but it's no use."

She chuckled grimly. "Then you don't read all that's in Granny's mind. Granny's no fool. Granny's smart; and she knows better than to think she can force a slan to stay and work for her. He has to be free for what she wants him to do. He's got to see that, being a slan, this will be the safest place for him until he grows up. Now, isn't Granny clever?"

Jommy sighed sleepily. "I can see what's in your mind, but I can't talk to you now. When we slans are sick—and that's not often—we just sleep and sleep. My waking up the way I did means that my subconscious was worried and forced me awake because it thought I was in danger. We slans have a lot of protections like that. But now I've got to go back to sleep and get well."

The coal-black eyes grew wide. The lustful mind recoiled, briefly accepting defeat in its main purpose of making immediate wealth from its prey. Greed yielded momentarily to violent curiosity, but there was no intention of letting him sleep.

"Is it true that slans make monsters out of human beings?"

Fury burned through Jommy's brain. Weariness fell away from him. He sat up, in rage.

"That's a lie! It's one of those horrible lies that human beings

32

tell about us to make us seem inhuman, to make everybody hate us, kill us. It—"

He sank back, exhausted, rage evaporating. "My mother and father were the finest people alive," he said softly, "and they were terribly unhappy. They met on the street one day, and saw in each other's minds that they were slans. Until then they'd lived the loneliest of lives, they'd never harmed anyone. It's the human beings who are the criminals. Dad didn't fight as hard as he could have when they cornered him and shot him in the back. He could have fought. He should have! Because he had the most terrible weapon the world has ever seen—so terrible he wouldn't even carry it with him for fear he might use it. When I'm fifteen I'm supposed to—"

He stopped, appalled at his indiscretion. For an instant he felt so sick, so weary, that his mind refused to hold the burden of his thought. He knew only that he had given away the greatest secret in slan history, and if this grasping old wretch turned him over to the police in his present weakened condition, all was lost.

Slowly, he breathed easier. He saw that her mind hadn't really caught the enormous implication in his revelation. She hadn't really heard him at the moment when he mentioned the weapon —for that rapacious brain had already been too long away from its main purpose. And now, like a vulture, it swooped down on prey it knew to be exhausted.

"Granny's glad to know that Jommy's such a nice boy. Poor, starving old Granny needs a young slan to make money for her and him. You won't mind working for tired old Granny, will you?" Her voice hardened. "Beggars can't be choosers, you know."

The knowledge that his secret was safe acted like a drug. His eyelids drooped. He said, "Really, I can't talk to you now; I've got to sleep."

He saw that she wasn't going to let him go. Her mind had already realized what could agitate him. She spoke sharply, not because she was interested, but to keep him awake.

"What is a slan? What makes you different? Where did slans come from in the first place? They were made, weren't they— like machines?"

Funny how that could bring a surge of responsive anger when his mind saw that that was her purpose. Dimly he realized that bodily weakness had taken normal restraints from his mind. He said in a dull rage, "That's another of the lies. I was born just like anyone else. So were my parents. Beyond that, I don't know."

"Your parents must have known!" the old woman prodded him.

Jommy shook his head. His eyes closed. "No, Mother said Dad was always too busy to investigate the mystery of the slans.

But now, leave me alone. I know what you're trying to do and I know what you want, but it's dishonest and I won't do it."

"That's stupid," the old woman snapped angrily, on her subject at last. "Is it dishonest to rob people who live by robbery and cheating? Shall you and Granny eat crusts of bread when the world is so rich that every treasury bulges with gold, every granary bulges with wheat, and honey flows in the streets? Bah for your honesty! That's what Granny says. How can a slan, hunted like a rat, talk of being honest?"

Jommy was silent and not only because of his need for sleep. He had had thoughts like that himself. The old woman pounded on:

"Where will you go? What will you do? Will you live in the streets? What about winter? Where in all this world can a little slan boy go?"

Her voice sank, in an attempt at sympathy. "Your poor, dear mother would have wanted you to do what I'm asking. She had no love for human beings. I've saved the paper to show you how they shot her down like a dog when she tried to escape. Would you like to see it?"

"No!" said Jommy, but his mind whirled.

The harsh voice pressed on. "Don't you want to do everything you can against a world that's so cruel? Make them pay? Make them regret what they've done? You're not afraid?"

He was silent. The old woman's voice took on a whine. "Life's too hard for old Granny—too hard. If you won't help Granny, she'll have to go on doing other things. You saw in her mind about them. But she promises not to do that any more if you'll help her. Think of that. She'll stop all the wicked things she's had to do for a living in this cold, cruel world."

Jommy felt beaten. He said slowly, "You're a rotten, miserable old scoundrel, and someday I'll kill you!"

"Then you'll stay until that 'someday'," Granny said triumphantly. Her wrinkled fingers rubbed together like dry scaled snakes crawling over each other. "And you'll do as Granny says, too, or she'll turn you over to the police so fast— Welcome to our little home, Jommy. Welcome. You'll be better the next time you waken, Granny hopes."

"Yes," Jommy said weakly. "I'll be better."

He slept.

Three days later, Jommy followed the old woman through the kitchen toward the back door. The kitchen was a bare little room, and Jommy closed his mind against the dirt and untidiness. He thought: The old woman was right. Horrible as the life promised to be, this shack, sunk here in the oblivion of poverty, would make an ideal retreat for a slan boy who had to wait at least six years before he could visit the hiding place of his father's secrets;

who had to grow up before he could hope to carry out the great things that had to be done.

The thought flew as the door opened and he saw what lay beyond. He stopped short, stunned by the vista that opened up before him. Never in all the world had he expected to see anything like *this*.

First was the yard, piled with old metal and junk of every description. A yard barren of grass or trees, without beauty; a discordant, jangling stretch of sterility enclosed by a rusting, twisted fence of rotten wood and wire. A small, ramshackle barn tottered precariously at the farthest end of the yard. The blurred mind pictures of a horse came from inside. The horse itself was visible through the open door.

But Jommy's eyes flashed past the yard. His passing glance picked up the unpleasant details; that was all. His mind, his vision, reached beyond the fence, beyond that rickety barn. Beyond, there were trees, little groups of them; and grass—a green, pleasant meadow that sloped toward a broad river, gleaming dully now that the rays of the sun no longer touched it with their shining fire.

But even the meadow (part of a golf course, he noted absently) held his gaze for an instant only. A land of dream began on the opposite shore of the river, a veritable fairyland of growth, a gardener's paradise. Because of some trees that blocked his vision, he could see only a narrow stretch of that Eden, with its sparkling fountains and its square mile on square mile of flowers and terraces and beauty. But that narrow, visible area contained a white pathway.

A pathway! Jommy's mind soared. Unutterable emotion choked his throat. The path was visible, running in a geometrically straight line away from his gaze. It ran into the dim distance, a gleaming ribbon that faded into the mist of miles. And it was there, at the ultimate limit of his vision, far beyond the normal horizon, that he saw the palace.

Only part of the base of that tremendous, that incredible structure reached up from the other side of the skyline. A thousand feet it reared and then it merged into a tower that soared another five hundred feet into the heavens. Stupendous tower! Half a thousand feet of jewel-like lacework that seemed almost fragile, sparkling there with all the colours of the rainbow, a translucent, shining, fantastic thing, built in the noble style of the old days; not merely ornamental—in its very design, its fine-wrought magnificence, it was ornament in itself.

Here in this glory of architectural triumph the slans had created their masterpiece, only to have it fall to the victors after the war of disaster.

It was too beautiful. It hurt his eyes, hurt his mind with the thoughts that it brought. To think that he had lived so close to this city for nine years and had never before seen this glorious achievement of his race! His mother's reason for not showing it to him seemed mistaken, now that he had the reality before him. "It'll make you bitter, Jommy, to realize that the palace of the slans now belongs to Kier Gray and his ghoulish crew. Besides, there are special precautions against us at that end of the city. You'll see it soon enough."

But it wasn't soon enough. The sense of something missed burned bright and painful. It would have given him courage in his blacker moments to know of this noble monument to his people.

His mother had said, "Human beings will never know all the secrets of that building. There are mysteries there, forgotten rooms and passages, hidden wonders that even the slans no longer know about, except in a vague way. Kier Gray doesn't realize it, but all the weapons and machines the human beings have searched for so desperately are buried right in that building."

A harsh voice jarred his ears. Jommy tore his gaze reluctantly from the grandeur across the river and became aware of Granny. He saw she had hitched the old horse to her junk wagon.

"Quit your daydreaming," she commanded. "And don't get any funny ideas into your head. The palace and palace grounds are not for slans. And now, get in under these blankets, and keep your mind still. There's a busybody policeman up the street who'd better not find out about you yet. We've got to hurry."

Jommy's eyes turned to the palace for one last lingering look. So that palace wasn't for slans! He felt a queer thrill. Someday he'd go over there to look for Kier Gray. And when that day came— The thought stopped; he was trembling with rage and hatred against the men who had murdered his father and his mother.

5

THE RICKETY OLD CART was downtown now. It rattled and shook over the uneven pavement of the back alleys until Jommy, half lying, half crouching in the back, felt as if he would be shaken out of his clothes. Twice he attempted to stand up, but each time the old woman poked at him with her stick.

"You stay down! Granny doesn't want anyone to see those fine clothes of yours. You just keep covered up with that robe."

The tattered old robe stank of Bill, the horse. The stench brought Jommy moments of nausea. At long last the junk wagon stopped.

"Get out," snapped Granny, "and go into that department store. You'll find big pockets I've sewn inside your coat. Just fill them with stuff so they won't bulge."

Dizzily, Jommy climbed down to the concrete. He stood there swaying, waiting for the swift flame of his strength to drive away that abnormal weakness. He said then, "I'll be back in about half an hour."

Her rapacious face bent toward him. Her black eyes glittered. "And don't get caught, and use your common sense in what you take."

"You needn't worry," Jommy replied confidently. "Before I take anything, I'll throw my mind around to see if anyone is looking. It's as simple as that."

"Good!" The thin face broke into a grin. "And don't worry if Granny isn't here when you come back. She's going over to the liquor store for some medicine. She can afford medicine now that she's got a young slan; and she does need it—oh, so much— to warm her cold old bones. Yes, Granny must lay in a good supply of medicine."

Outside fear came rushing in to him as he breasted the throngs that washed in and out of the skyscraper department store; abnormal, exaggerated fear. He opened his mind wide, and for one long moment kept it that way. Excitement, tenseness, dismay and uncertainty—an enormous, dark spray of fear caught at him and twisted his mind along into the swirling stream of it. Shuddering, he pulled himself clear.

But during that plunge he had caught the basis of that mass fear. Executions at the palace! John Petty, the head of the secret police, had caught ten councillors making a deal with the slans, and killed them. The crowd didn't quite believe. They were afraid of John Petty. They distrusted him. Thank heaven Kier Gray was there, solid as a rock to protect the world from the slans—and from the sinister John Petty.

It was worse inside the store. There were more people. Their thoughts pounded at his brain as he threaded his way along the aisles of shining floor displays, under the gleam of the ceiling lights. A gorgeous world of goods in enormous quantities swelled all around him, and taking what he wanted proved easier than he had expected.

He passed the end of the long, glittering jewellery department and helped himself to a pendant marked fifty-five dollars. His impulse was to enter the department, but he caught the thought of the salesgirl. Annoyance was in her mind, hostility at the idea of a small boy entering the jewellery section. Children were not welcome in that world of magnificent gems and fine metals.

Jommy turned away, brushing past a tall, good-looking man who whisked by without so much as a glance at him. Jommy walked on for a few paces, and stopped. A shock such as he had never known before stabbed through him. It was like a knife cutting into his brain, it was so sharp. And yet it was not unpleasant. Astonishment, joy, amazement flashed through him as he turned and stared eagerly after the retreating man.

The handsome, powerfully built stranger was a slan, a full-grown slan! The discovery was so important that, after the first realization sank in, his brain reeled. The basic calm of his slan-steady mind was not shattered, nor was there the sinking into emotionalism that he had noticed when he was sick. But his mind soared with a sheer, wild eagerness unequalled in his past experience.

He began to walk rapidly after the man. His thought reached out, seeking contact with the other's brain—recoiled! Jommy frowned. He could still see that the being was a slan, but he could not penetrate beyond the surface of the stranger's mind. And that surface reflected no awareness of Jommy, not the faintest suggestion that he was conscious of any outside thoughts at all.

There was mystery here. It had been impossible a few days before to read beyond the surface of John Petty's mind. Yet there had never been any question of Petty being anything but a human being. It was impossible to explain the difference to himself. Except that when his mother guarded her thoughts from intrusion, he had always been able to make her aware with a directed vibration.

The conclusion was staggering. It meant that here was a slan who couldn't read minds, yet guarded his own brain from being read. Guarded it from whom? From other slans? And what manner of slan was it that couldn't read minds? They were out in the street now; and it would have been easy, there under the brilliant lights that blazed from the street lamps, to break into a run that would have brought him up to the slan in a few moments. In all those rushing, selfish crowds, who would notice a little boy running?

But instead of narrowing the gap that separated him from the slan, he allowed it to widen. The entire logical roots of his existence were threatened by the situation presented by this slan; and the whole hypnotic education that his father had imprinted upon his mind rose up and prevented precipitant action.

Two blocks from the store, the slan turned up a wide, side street; puzzled, Jommy followed him at a safe distance—puzzled, because he knew this was something of a dead-end street, not a residential section. One, two, three blocks they went. And then he was certain.

The slan was heading for the Air Centre that, with all its buildings and factories and landing field, sprawled for a square mile at this part of the city. The thing was impossible. Why, people couldn't even get near an airplane without having to remove their hats to prove that they were minus slan tendrils.

The slan headed straight toward a big, blazing sign: AIR CENTRE—vanished without hesitation into the revolving door under the sign.

Jommy paused at the door. *The Air Centre, which dominated the entire aircraft industry on the face of the globe!* Was it possible that slans worked here? That in the very centre of the human world that hated them with almost unimaginable ferocity slans actually controlled the greatest transportation system in the entire world?

He pushed through the door, and along the corridor of marble that stretched ahead of him, countless doors leading off it. For the moment there was not a person in sight, but little thoughts trickled out to feed his growing amazement and delight.

The place swarmed with slans. There must be scores, *hundreds*!

Just ahead of him, a door opened, and two bareheaded young men came out and walked toward him. They were talking quietly to each other, and for a moment did not see him. He had time to catch their surface thoughts, the calm and magnificent confidence of them, the lack of fear. Two slans, in the very prime of maturity—and bareheaded!

Bareheaded. That was what finally penetrated to Jommy above everything else. Bareheaded—and without tendrils.

For a moment it seemed to him that his eyes must be playing him tricks. His gaze searched almost frantically for the golden strands of tendril that should have been there. Tendrilless slans!

So that was it! That explained why they couldn't read minds. The men were only ten feet away from him, and simultaneously, they became aware of him. They stopped.

"Boy," said one, "you'll have to get out. Children are not allowed in here. Run along now."

Jommy drew a deep breath. The mildness of the reproof was reassuring, especially now that the mystery was explained. It was wonderful that, by the simple removal of their telltale tendrils, they could live and work securely in the very centre of their enemies! With a sweeping, almost melodramatic gesture, he reached up to his cap, and removed it. "It's all right," he began. "I'm—"

The words blurred on his lips. He watched the two men with fear-widened eyes. For after one uncontrolled moment of surprise, their mind shields closed tight. Their smiles were friendly. One said, "Well, this is a surprise!"

And the other echoed, "A damned pleasant surprise. Welcome, kid!"

But Jommy was not listening. His mind was swaying from the shock of the thoughts that had exploded in the brains of the two men in that brief period when they saw the glittering golden tendrils in his hair:

"God," the first one thought, "it's a snake!"

And from the other came a thought utterly cold, utterly merciless: "Kill the damned thing!"

6

FOR JOMMY, from the moment he caught the thoughts of the two slans, it was not a question of what he should do but whether he had time to do it. Even the devastating surprise of their murderous enmity did not basically affect his actions or his brain.

He knew, without even thinking about it, that to run back along the corridors, trying to cover the hundred yards of straight-away marble floors, would be suicide. His nine-year-old legs could never match the tireless endurance of two able-bodied slans. There was only one thing to do, and he did it. With a boy's agility, he twisted to one side. There was a door there, one of the hundreds that lined the corridor.

Fortunately, it was unlocked. Before his battering rush it opened with surprising ease, yet so careful was his control that the actual opening he allowed himself was only barely large enough for him to slip through. He had a glimpse of a second lighted corridor, empty of life; and then he was shutting the door, his strong, brown, sensitive fingers fumbling at the lock. The latch and the lock clicked home with a sharp, hard, thrilling sound.

The very next instant there was a violent thud as two adult bodies dashed themselves against the barrier. But the door did not even tremble.

Jommy realized the truth. The door was of solid metal, built to withstand battering-rams, yet so wonderfully balanced that it had appeared weightless to his fingers. For the moment, he was safe!

His mind relaxed from its concentration and reached for contact with the minds of the two slans. At first it seemed as if their shields were too tightly held, then his exploring brain caught the overtones of chagrin and an anxiety so terrible that it was like a knife hacking at the surface of their thoughts.

"God almighty!" one whispered. "Sound the secret alarm, quick! If the snakes find out we control Airways—"

Jommy wasted not another second. Every atom of curiosity in him was driving him to stay, to solve the bewildering hatred of the tendrilless slan for the true slan. But before the dictates of common sense, curiosity retreated. He ran at top speed, sure of what he must do.

He knew that by no logic could that gauntlet of corridor be considered safe. At any moment a door might open, or wisps of thought warn him of men coming around some bend. With abrupt decision, he slowed his headlong rush and tried several doors. The fourth door yielded to pressure, and Jommy crossed the threshold with a sense of triumph. On the far side of the room was a tall, broad window.

He pushed the window open and scrambled out onto the wide sill. Crouching low, he peered over the ledge. Light came dimly from the other windows of the building, and by its glow he could see what appeared to be a narrow driveway wedged between two precipices of brick wall.

For an instant he hesitated and then, like a human fly, started up the brick wall. The climbing was simple enough; enormously strong fingers searched with swift sureness for rough edges. The deepening darkness, as he climbed, was hampering, but with every upward step his confidence surged stronger within him. There were miles of roof here and, if he remembered rightly, the airport buildings connected on every side with other buildings. What chance had slans who could not read minds against a slan who could avoid their every trap?

The thirtieth, and top, storey! With a sigh of relief, Jommy pulled himself erect and started along the flat roof. It was nearly dark now, but he could see the top of a neighbouring building that almost touched the roof he was on. A leap of two yards at most, an easy jump. With a loud *clang*! the clock in a near-by tower began to intone the hour. One—two—five—ten! And on the stroke, a low, grinding noise struck Jommy's ears, and suddenly, in the shadowy centre of that expanse of roof opposite him yawned a wide, black hole. Startled, he flung himself flat, holding his breath.

And from that dark hole a dim torpedolike shape leaped into the star-filled sky. Faster, faster it went; and then, at the uttermost limit of vision, a tiny, blazing light sprang from its rear. It flickered there for a moment, then was gone, like a star snuffed out.

Jommy lay very still, his eyes straining to follow the path of the strange craft. A spaceship. By all the heavens, a spaceship! Had these tendrilless slans realized the dream of the ages—to operate flights to the planets? If so, how had they kept it secret from human beings? And what were the true slans doing?

The scraping noise reached him again. He crept to the edge of the roof and peered across. He could only vaguely see the yawning blackness lessen as the two great metal sheets slid together and the roof was whole again.

For a moment longer Jommy waited, then he bunched his muscles and sprang. Only one purpose was in his mind now: to get back to Granny quickly and by as devious a way as possible. Back alleys, side streets, must be his route. For this ease of escape from *slans* suddenly seemed suspicious. Unless, of course, they didn't dare set up safeguards for fear of betraying their secret to human beings.

Whatever the reason, it was only too obvious that he still needed desperately the security of Granny's little shack. He had no desire to tackle a problem so complicated and murderous as the slan-human-tendrilless slan triangle had become. No, not until he was full-grown and capable of matching the sharp brains that were fighting this unceasing and deadly battle.

Yes, back to Granny, and by way of the store to get some peace offerings for the old wretch, now that he was certain to be late. And he'd have to hurry, too. The store would close at eleven.

At the store, Jommy did not venture near the jewellery counter, for the girl who objected to little boys was still at work. There were other richly laden counters, and he swiftly skimmed the cream of their smaller merchandise. Nevertheless, he made a mental note that, if he came into this store in future, he would have to be on the scene before five o'clock, when the evening staff arrived for their shift. Otherwise that girl could prove a nuisance.

Sated at last with stolen goods, he headed cautiously for the nearest exit, then stopped as a man, a middle-aged, paunchy person, walked by thoughtfully. The man was the chief accountant of the store, and he was thinking of the four hundred thousand dollars that would be in the safe overnight. In his mind, also, was the combination of the safe.

Jommy hurried on, but he was disgusted with his lack of foresight. How foolish to steal goods that would have to be sold, with the risks at both ends enormous compared to the simple business of taking all the money he wanted.

Granny was still where he had left her, but her mind was in such turmoil that he had to wait for her to speak before he could understand what she wanted.

"Quick," she said hoarsely, "get in under the blankets. A policeman was just here warning Granny to move on."

It must have been at least a mile farther on that she stopped the cart and tore the blanket off Jommy with a snarl. "You ungrateful wretch, where have you been?"

Jommy wasted no words. His contempt was too great for him to speak to her more than he had to. He shivered as he watched the eagerness with which she snatched at the treasure he dumped into her lap. Swiftly she evaluated each item, and stuffed it carefully into the false bottom that had been built into the cart.

"At least two hundred dollars for old Granny!" she said joyously. "Old Finn will give Granny that much. Oh, but Granny's smart, catching a young slan. He'll make not ten thousand but twenty thousand a year for her. And to think they offered only ten thousand dollars' reward! It should be a million."

"I can do even better than that," Jommy volunteered. It seemed as good a time as any to tell her about the store safe, and that there was no need for more shoplifting. "There's about four thousand in the safe," he finished. "I can get it tonight. I'll climb up the back of the building, where it's dark, to one of the windows, cut a hole in it . . . you've got a glass cutter somewhere?"

"Granny can get one!" the old woman breathed ecstatically. She rocked back and forth with joy. "Oh, oh, Granny's glad. But Granny can see now why human beings shoot slans. They're too dangerous. Why, they could steal the world. They tried to, you know, in the beginning."

"I don't . . . know . . . very much about that," Jommy said slowly. He wished desperately that Granny knew all about it, but he saw that she didn't. There was only the vaguest knowledge in her mind of that misty period when the slans (so human beings accused) had tried to conquer the world. She knew no more than he did, no more than all this vast ignorant mass of people.

What was the truth? Had there ever been a war between slans and human beings? Or was it just the same propaganda as that dreadful stuff about what slans did to babies? Jommy saw that Granny's mind had jumped back to the money in the store.

"Only four thousand dollars!" she said sharply. "Why, they must make hundreds of thousands every day—millions!"

"They don't keep it all in the store," lied Jommy, and to his relief the old woman accepted the explanation.

He thought about the lie as the cart rattled on. He had uttered it in the first place almost automatically. Now he saw that it was self-protection. If he made the old woman too rich, she would soon begin to think of betraying him.

It was absolutely imperative that during the next six years he live in the security of Granny's shack. The question therefore became: How little would she be satisfied with? Somewhere he must strike a mean between her insatiable greed and his necessity.

Just thinking about that enlarged its dangers. In this woman was an incredible selfishness, and a streak of cowardice that might surge in a panic of fear and destroy him before he could properly realize his danger.

No doubt about it. Among the known imponderables overhanging the precious six years separating him from his father's mighty science, this gaunt rascal loomed as the most dangerous and the most uncertain factor.

7

THE ACQUISITION OF MONEY corrupted Granny. She disappeared for days at a time, and he gathered from her disjointed conversation afterwards that she was at last frequenting the pleasure resorts she had always longed to go to. When she was at home, her bottle was her almost inseparable companion. Because he needed to have her around, Jommy prepared meals for her, and so kept her alive despite her excesses. It was necessary—when she ran out of money—to make occasional forays with her, but otherwise he kept effectively out of her way.

He used his considerable spare time to gain an education—something which was not easy to do. The area was poverty-stricken in the extreme, and most of its inhabitants were uneducated, even illiterate, but there was a scattering of people with alert minds in it. Jommy discovered who they were and what they did and how much they knew by asking them and by asking about them. To them, he was Granny's grandson. Once that was accepted as fact, many difficulties were resolved.

There were people, of course, who were wary of a junk dealer's relative, considering him untrustworthy. A few individuals, who had felt the sting of Granny's sharp tongue, were quite antagonistic; but their reaction was to ignore him. Others were too busy to bother with either Granny or himself.

From some he aggressively, though as unobtrusively as possible, compelled attention. A young engineering student called him "a damned nuisance," but explained the science of engineering to him. Jommy read in his mind that the student felt that he was clarifying his own thoughts and understanding of his subject, and that he occasionally boasted that he knew engineering so well that he could make the principles clear to a boy of ten.

He never guessed how precocious this boy was.

A woman who had travelled widely before her marriage—but was now in poor circumstances—lived half a block down the street, and fed him cookies one at a time while she talked eagerly of the world and its people as she had seen them.

It was necessary to accept the bribes because she would have misunderstood if he refused the cookies. But no teller of tales actually ever had a more attentive pair of ears to talk to than Mrs. Hardy. A thin-faced, bitter woman whose husband had gambled away her possessions, she had wandered over Europe and Asia, and her sharp eyes had recorded an immense amount of detail. More vaguely, she knew about the past of those countries.

At one time—so she had heard—China had been heavily populated. The story was that a series of bloody wars had long ago decimated the more densely inhabited areas. These wars, it seemed, were definitely not of slan origin. It was only in the last hundred years that the slans had turned their attention to babies of Chinese and other Eastern origin—and so turned against them people who had hitherto tolerated the slans' existence.

As explained by Mrs. Hardy, it seemed like one more senseless action of the slans. Jommy listened and recorded the information, convinced that the explanation could not be as stated, wondering what the truth was, and determined that someday he would bring all these deadly lies out into the open.

The engineering student, Mrs. Hardy, a grocer who had been a rocket pilot, a radio and TV repairman, and Old Man Darrett—these were the people who educated him, unknowingly, during the first two years he spent with Granny. Of the group, Darrett was Jommy's prize. A big, stocky, lonely, cynical man of seventy-odd years, he had once been a professor of history—but that was merely one of the many subjects about which he had an almost inexhaustible fund of information.

It was obvious that sooner or later the old man would bring up the subject of the slan wars. It was so obvious that Jommy allowed the first few casual mentions of it to pass, just as if he weren't interested. But early one winter afternoon, there it was again, as he had expected. And this time he said:

"You keep talking about wars. There couldn't have been wars. Those people are just outlaws. You don't fight wars with outlaws; you just exterminate them."

Darrett stiffened. "Outlaws," he said. "Young fellow, those were great days. I tell you a hundred thousand slans practically took over the world. It was a beautiful job of planning, carried out with the utmost boldness. What you have to realize is that men as a mass always play somebody else's game—not their own. They're caught in traps from which they cannot escape. They belong to groups; they're members of organizations; they're loyal to ideas, individuals, geographical areas. If you can get hold of the institutions they support—there's the method."

"And the slans did *that*?" Jommy asked the question with an intensity that startled him; it was a little too revealing of his own feelings. He added quickly in a subdued tone: "It sounds like a story. It's just propaganda to scare us—like you've said so often about other things."

"Propaganda!" said Darrett explosively. And then he was silent. His large, expressive black eyes were half hidden by his long, dark eyelashes. He said at last slowly, "I want you to

46

visualize this, Jommy. The world was confused and bewildered. Everywhere human babies were being subjected to the tremendous campaign of the slans to make more slans. Civilization began to break down. There was an immense increase in insanity. Suicide, murder, crime—the graph of chaos rose to new heights. And, one morning, without knowing quite how it was done, the human race woke up to discover that overnight the enemy had taken control. Working from within, the slans had managed to take over innumerable key organizations. When you learn to understand the rigidity of institutional structures in our society, you'll realize how helpless human beings were at first. My own private opinion is that the slans could have gotten away with it except for one thing."

Jommy waited, silent. He had an unhappy premonition of what was coming. Old Man Darrett went on:

"They continued ruthlessly trying to make slans out of human babies. It seems a little stupid in retrospect."

Darrett and the others were only the beginning. He followed learned men around the streets, picking at the surface of their minds. He lay in concealment on campus grounds, telepathically following lectures. Books he had in plenty, but books were not enough. They had to be interpreted, explained. There were mathematics, physics, chemistry, astronomy—all the sciences. His desire had no limit.

In the six years between his ninth and fifteenth birthdays, he acquired the beginning of what his mother had prescribed as basic knowledge for an adult slan.

During those years, he watched the tendrilless slans cautiously from a distance. Nightly, at ten, their spaceships leaped into the sky; and the service was maintained on precision time. Every night at two-thirty, another shark-shaped monster plunged down from space, silent and dark, and dropped like a ghost into the top of the same building.

Only twice during those years was the traffic suspended, each time for a month, and each time when Mars, following her eccentric orbit, teetered on the farthest side of the Sun.

He stayed away from the Air Centre, because almost every day his respect for the might of the tendrilless slans grew. And it seemed increasingly clear that only an accident had saved him that day when he revealed himself to the two adults. An accident and surprise.

Of the basic mysteries of the slans he learned nothing. To pass the time he indulged in orgies of physical activity. First of all, he must have a secret way of escape, just in case—secret from Granny as well as the world; and second, he couldn't possibly live in this shack as it was. It required months to build hundreds of yards of tunnel, months also to rebuild the interior of their home with fine, panelled walls, shining ceilings and plastic floors.

Granny sneaked the furniture in at night, past the junk-laden yard and the unchanged, unpainted exterior. But that required nearly a year in itself—because of Granny and her bottle.

His fifteenth birthday . . . At two in the afternoon, Jommy laid down the book he had been reading, took off his slippers and put on his shoes. The hour for decisive action had come. Today, he must go into the catacombs, and take possession of his father's secret. Because he did not know the secret slan passageways, he would have to risk going in through a public entrance.

He gave scarcely more than a surface thought to the possibility of danger. This was the day—long ago, it had been planted in his mind, hypnotically set by his father. It did seem important, however, that he slip out of the house without the old woman's hearing him.

Briefly, he let his mind contact hers, and without the slightest sense of disgust sampled the stream of her thought. She was wide awake and tossing on her bed. And through her brain poured freely and furiously a welter of astoundingly wicked thoughts.

Jommy Cross frowned abruptly. Into the veritable hell of the old woman's recollection (for she lived almost completely in her amazing past when she was drunk) had come a swift, cunning thought: "Got to get rid of that slan . . . dangerous for Granny now that she's got money. Mustn't let him suspect . . . keep it out of my mind so . . ."

Jommy Cross smiled mirthlessly. It was not the first time he had caught the thought of treachery in her brain. With sudden purposefulness he finished tying the shoelace, stood up and went into her room.

Granny lay, a sprawling shape under the sheets that were stained brown with liquor. Her deeply sunken black eyes stared dully out of the wrinkled parchment of her face. Gazing down at her, Jommy Cross felt a quiver of pity. Terrible and vicious as had been the old Granny, he preferred her as she had been then to this weak old soak who lay like some medieval witch miraculously deposited in a blue and silver bed of the future.

Her eyes seemed to see him for the first time, clearly. A string of bloodthirsty curses reeled from her lips. Then, "Waddya want? Granny wants to be alone."

The pity drained out of him. He gazed at her coldly: "I just wanted to give you a little warning. I'm leaving soon, so you won't have to spend any more time thinking of ways to betray me. There aren't any safe ways. That treasured old hide of yours wouldn't be worth a nickel if they caught me."

The black eyes gleamed up at him slyly. "Think you're smart, eh," she mumbled. The word seemed to start a new trend of

48

thought that it was impossible for him to follow mentally. "Smart," she repeated gloatingly, "smartest thing Granny ever did, catching a young slan. Dangerous now though . . . got to get rid of him . . ."

"You old fool," Jommy Cross said dispassionately. "Don't forget that a person who harbours a slan is automatically subject to death. You've kept that mud-turtle-complexioned neck of yours well oiled, so it probably won't squeal when they hang you, but you'll do plenty of kicking with those scrawny legs."

The brutal words spoken, he turned abruptly and went out of the room, out of the house. On the bus, he thought: "I've got to watch her, and as soon as possible leave her. Nobody who thinks in probabilities could trust anything valuable to *her*."

Even downtown, the streets were deserted. Jommy Cross climbed off the bus, conscious of the silence where usually there was bedlam. The city was too quiet; there was a very absence of life and movement. He stood uncertainly at the curb, all thought of Granny draining from him. He opened his mind wide. At first there was nothing there but a wisp from the half-blank mind of the driver of the bus which was disappearing now down the otherwise carless road. The sun glared down on the pavement. A few people scuttled hurriedly past, in their minds simply a blank terror so continuous and unvarying that he could not penetrate beyond it.

The silence deepened, and alarm crept into Jommy Cross. He explored the buildings around him, but no clamour of minds came from them, nothing whatever. The clatter of an engine burst abruptly from a side street. Two blocks away a tractor emerged, pulling a tremendous gun that pointed menacingly into the sky. The tractor clattered into the centre of the street, was unhooked from the gun, and bellowed off into the side street from which it had come. Men swarmed around the gun, preparing it, and then stood by, looking up at the sky, waiting tensely.

Jommy Cross wanted to walk closer, to read their minds, but he didn't dare. The sense of being in an exposed and dangerous position grew into a sick conviction within him. Any minute a military or police car might roll past and its occupants ask him what he was doing in the street. He might be arrested, or told to take off his cap and show his hair and the golden threads that were his tendrils.

Something big was definitely up, and the best place for him was the catacombs, where he'd be out of sight, though in a different kind of danger. He started hurriedly toward the catacomb entrance that had been his goal ever since leaving the house. He was turning into a side street when the loud-speaker at the corner blared into life. A man's voice roared hoarsely:

"Final warning—*get off the street*! Get out of sight. The mysterious airship of the slans is now approaching the city at terrific speed. It is believed the ship is heading toward the palace. Interference has been set up on all radio waves, to prevent any of the slan lies from being broadcast. Get off the streets! *Here comes the ship!*"

Jommy froze. There was a silver flash in the sky, and then a long, winged torpedo of glittering metal hurtled by straight above. He heard a staccato roar from the gun down the street, and the echo of other guns, and then the ship was a distant sparkling point, heading toward the palace.

Curiously, the sun's glare hurt his eyes now. He was conscious of confusion. *A winged ship!* Scores of nights during these past six years he had watched the spaceships soar up from the building in the tendrilless slan Air Centre. Wingless rocket ships, and something more. Something that made great metal machines lighter than air. The rocket part seemed to be used only for propulsion. The weightlessness, the way they were flung up as if by centrifugal force, *must* be antigravity! And here was a *winged* ship, with all that that implied; jet engines, rigid confinement to Earth's atmosphere, ordinariness. If this was the best the true slans could do, then—

Sharply disappointed, he turned and walked down the long flight of stairs that led to the public washroom. The place was as empty and silent as the streets above. And it was a simple matter for him who had passed through so many locked doors to pick the lock of the steel-barred door leading to the catacombs.

He was conscious of the tenseness of his mind as he stared through the bars of the door. There was a vague foreground of concrete beyond, then a blur of darkness that meant more stairs. The muscles of his throat tightened, his breath became deep and slow. He hunched his slim length forward, like a runner getting ready for a sprint. He opened the door, darted inside, and down the long reach of dark, dank steps at top speed.

Somewhere ahead, a bell began ringing monotonously, set off by the photoelectric cells whose barrier Jommy had crossed on entering the door—a protection put up years ago against slans and other interlopers.

The bell was just a short distance away now, and still there was no mind stirring out of the corridor that yawned before him. Apparently none of the men working or on guard in the catacombs was within hearing range. He saw the bell, high up on the wall, a glimmering piece of metal, *brrring* noisily. The wall was smooth as glass, impossible to climb, the bell more than twelve feet from the floor. On and on it clanged, and still there was no clamour of approaching minds, not the faintest wisp of thought.

"No proof that they're not coming," Jommy thought tensely. "These stone walls would quickly diffuse thought waves."

He took a run at the wall, and leaped with desperate strength, up, up, toward the instrument. His arm strained, his fingers scraped the marble wall, a full foot below the bell. He fell back, knowing his defeat. It was still ringing as he rounded a bend in the corridor. He heard it grow fainter and fainter, fading into the distance behind him. But even after the sound was gone, the ghost of it went on ringing in his mind, an insistent warning of danger.

Queerly, the sense of a warning buzz in his brain grew stronger, until suddenly it seemed to him that the bell was actually there again, faint with distance. The feeling grew stronger, until abruptly he realized that there was another bell, clanging as noisily as the first one. That meant (he felt appalled) there must be a long line of such bells sending out their alarms, and somewhere in that vast network of tunnels there must be ears to hear them, men stiffening and looking at each other with narrowed eyes.

Jommy Cross hurried on. He had no conscious knowledge of his route. He knew only that his father had hypnotized a picture of it into his mind, and that he need but follow the promptings of his subconscious. It came abruptly, a sharp mental command: "To the right!"

He took the narrower of the two forks—and came at last to the hiding place. It was all simple enough, a cleverly loosened slab in the marble wall that slid out under the pressure of his strength, revealing a dark space beyond. He reached in; his groping fingers touched a metal box. He pulled it to him. He was shaking now, his fingers trembling. For a moment he stood very still, fighting for self-control; striving to picture his father standing here before this slab hiding his secrets for his son to find if anything went wrong with his own personal plans.

It seemed to Jommy that this might be a cosmic moment in the history of slans, this moment when the work of a dead father was passed on to a fifteen-year-old boy who had waited so many thousands of minutes and hours and days for this second to come.

The nostalgia fled from him abruptly as a mist of outside thought whispered into his mind. "Damn that bell!" somebody was thinking. "It's probably someone who ran down when the slan ship came, trying to get away from expected bombs."

"Yeah, but don't count on it. You know how strict they are about these catacombs. Whoever started that bell is still inside. We'd better turn in the alarm to police headquarters."

A third vibration came: "Maybe the guy's lost."

"Let him explain that," said the first man. "Let's head toward the first bell and keep our guns ready. Never know what it might be. With slans flying around in the sky these days, there could be some of them coming down here, for all we know."

Frantically, Jommy examined the metal box for the secret of its opening. His hypnotic command was to take out the contents and put the empty box back in the hole. In the face of that order, the thought of grabbing up the box and running never even entered his head.

There seemed to be no lock and no catch. And yet, there must be something to fasten the lid down—Hurry, hurry! In a few minutes the approaching men would be passing directly by the spot where he was now standing.

The dimness of the long concrete and marble corridors, the dank odours, the consciousness of the thick cords of electric wires that ran by overhead feeding millions of volts to the city above, the whole world of the catacombs around, and even memories of his past—these were the thoughts that raced through Jommy's mind, as he stared down at the metal box. There was a thought of drunken Granny, and of the mystery of the slans, and it all mixed together with the approaching footsteps of the men. He could hear them plainly now, three pairs of them, clumping toward him.

Silently, Jommy Cross tore at the cover of the box, his muscles tensed for the effort. He nearly lost his balance, so easily did the unfastened cover lift up.

He found himself staring down at a thick rod of metal that lay on top of a pile of papers. He felt no surprise at its being there. There was, instead, a faint relief at discovering intact something he had *known* was there. Obviously, more of his father's hypnotism.

The metal rod was a bulbous thing about two inches wide at the centre but narrowing down at the ends. One of the ends was roughened, unmistakably meant to give the hand a good grip. There was a little button at the foot of the bulb part, convenient for the thumb to press it. The whole instrument glowed ever so faintly with a light of its own. That glow and the diffused light from the corridor were just bright enough for him to read on the sheet of paper beneath.

> *This is the weapon. Use it only*
> *in case of absolute necessity.*

For a moment, Jommy Cross was so intent that he didn't realize the men were upon him. A flashlight glared.

"What the—" one of the men roared. "Hands up, you!"

It was his first real, personal danger in six long years, and it felt unreal. The slow thought crept into him that human beings were not very quick in their reflexes. And then he was reaching for the weapon in the box before him. Without conscious haste, he pressed the button.

If any of the men fired, the action was lost in the roar of white flame that flashed with inconceivable violence from the mouth of the tube of force. One moment they were alive, rough-built, looming shapes, threatening him; the next, they were gone, snuffed out by that burst of virulent fire.

Jommy looked down at his hand. It was trembling. And there was a sickness in him at the way he had smashed three lives out of existence. The blur before his vision straightened slowly, as his eyes recovered from the fiery dazzlement. As his gaze reached farther out from him, he saw that the corridor was completely empty. Not a bone, not a piece of flesh or clothing remained to show that there had ever been living beings in the vicinity. Part of the floor was hollowed out, where that scorching incandescence had seared a concavity. But the slight, smooth depression it made would never be noticed.

He forced his fingers to stop trembling; slowly the sick feeling crept out of him. There was no use feeling badly. Killing was a tough business, but these men would have dealt death to him without compunction, as men already had to his father and mother—and to countless other slans who had died miserably because of the lies these people kept feeding to each other, and swallowing without the slightest resistance. Damn them all!

For a moment, his emotions were violent. He thought: Was it possible that all slans grew bitter as they became older, and ceased feeling compunctions about the killing of human beings, just as human beings had no compunctions about murdering slans?

His gaze fell on the sheet upon which his father had written:

> ... the weapon. Use it only in
> case of absolute necessity.

Memory flooded him, of a thousand other instances of his parents' noble quality of understanding. He could still remember the night his father had said, "Remember this: no matter how strong the slans become, the problem of what to do with human beings remains a barrier to occupation of the world. Until that problem is settled with justice and psychological sanity, the use of force would be a black crime."

Jommy felt better. There was proof. His father hadn't even carried with him a replica of this weapon that might have saved him from his enemies. He had taken death before he would deal it.

Jommy Cross frowned. Nobility was all very well, and perhaps he had lived too long with human beings to be a true slan, but he couldn't escape the conviction that fighting was better than dying.

The thought stopped, alarm replacing it. There was no time to waste. He had to get out of here, and quickly! He slipped the gun into his coat pocket, swiftly caught up the papers in the box, jammed them into his pockets. Then tossing the now empty, useless box back into its hole, slid the stone into place. He raced down the corridor, along the way he had come, up the steps, and stopped short within sight of the washroom. A little while before, it had been empty and silent. Now, it was packed with men. He waited, poised yet indecisive, hoping their numbers would dwindle.

But men came in, and men went out, and there was no lessening of the crowd, no diminishing of the bedlam of noise and thought. Excitement, fear, worry; here were little men in whose brains thundered the realization that big things were happening. And the echo of that realization poured through the iron bars of the door to where Jommy waited in the dimness. In the distance, the bell was still ringing. Its unrelenting *brrr* of warning finally dictated the action he must take. Clutching the weapon in his pocket with one hand, Jommy stepped forward gingerly, and pushed the door open. He shut it behind him softly, tensed for the slightest sign of alarm.

But the packed mass of men paid him not the least attention as he shoved his way through them and went up to the street. The pavement level was alive with people. Crowds pressed along the sidewalks and on the thoroughfares. Police whistles shrilled, loud-speakers blared, but nothing could stem the anarchism of the mob. All transport was at a standstill. Sweating, cursing drivers left their cars standing in the middle of the street and joined listeners before the street radios that kept up a machine-gun barrage.

"Nothing is known for certain. No one knows exactly whether the slan ship landed at the palace or dropped a message and then disappeared. No one saw it land; no one saw it disappear. It is possible that it was shot down. Then again it is possible that at this moment the slans are in conference with Kier Gray at the palace. Rumour to that effect has already spread, in spite of the noncommittal statement issued a few minutes ago by Kier Gray himself. For the benefit of those who did not hear that statement, I will repeat it. Ladies and gentlemen, the statement of Kier Gray was as follows:

" 'Do not be excited or alarmed. The extraordinary appearance of the slan ship has not altered the respective positions of slans and human beings in the slightest degree. We control the situation absolutely. They can do nothing anywhere except what they have been doing, and that within rigid limitations. Human beings outnumber slans probably millions to one; and, under such circumstances, they will never dare come out in an open, organized campaign against us. So be easy in your hearts—'

"That, ladies and gentlemen, was the statement issued by Kier Gray after the momentous event of today. The Council has been in continuous session since that statement was issued. I repeat, nothing more is known for certain. It is not known whether the slan ship landed. No one from the city saw it disappear. No one except the authorities know exactly what happened, and you have just heard the only statement on the matter, given out by Kier Gray himself. Whether the slan ship was shot down or—"

The chatter went on and on. Over and over the statement of Kier Gray was repeated, the same accompanying rumours were given. It became a drone in the back of Jommy's head, a senseless roar from loud-speaker after loud-speaker, a monotony of noise. But he stayed on, waiting for some additional information, eager with the burning eagerness of fifteen long years of wanting to know about other slans.

Only slowly did the flame of his excitement die. Nothing new was reported, and at last he climbed aboard a bus and headed for home. Darkness was settling over the hot spring day. A tower clock showed seventeen minutes past seven.

He approached the little junk-laden yard with his usual caution. His mind reached inside the deceptive, tumble-down-looking cottage, and touched Granny's mind. He sighed. Still drunk! How the devil did that wrecked caricature of a body stand it? So much liquor should have dehydrated her system before this. He pushed open the door, entered and shut it behind him—and then stopped short!

His mind, still in casual contact with Granny's mind, was receiving a thought. The old woman had heard the door open and shut, and the sound had jogged her mind briefly.

"Mustn't let him know I phoned the police. Keep it out of my mind . . . can't have a slan around . . . dangerous to have a slan . . . police'll have the streets barred . . ."

8

KATHLEEN LAYTON clenched her fists into small, firm, brown knobs. Her slim young body quivered in revulsion as she recognized the thoughts that came at her from one of the corridors. Seventeen-year-old Davy Dinsmore was searching for her, coming toward the marble parapet where she stood staring out at the city, which was wrapped in the soft mists of the humid, hot, spring afternoon.

The mists shifted in ever-changing design. They became like fleecy clouds that half hid buildings, then smeared into a haze that held locked within its flimsy texture the faintest tinge of sky-blue.

Queerly, the looking hurt her eyes without actually being unpleasant. The coolness of the palace breathed out at her from all the open doors, and beat back the heat of the sun. The glare remained, however.

The wisps of thought from Davy Dinsmore grew stronger, nearer. He was, she saw in his mind, going to try again to persuade her to be his girl friend. With a final shudder, Kathleen shut out his thoughts, and waited for the youth to appear. It had been a mistake to be polite to him, even though she had saved herself a lot of trouble during her early teens by having his support against the other young people. Now, she preferred his enmity to the type of love thoughts that permeated his brain.

"Oh," said Davy Dinsmore, emerging from a door, "here you are."

She stared at him without smiling. Davy Dinsmore at seventeen was a gangling youth, resembling in face his long-jawed mother, who always seemed to be sneering even when she smiled. He came up with an aggressiveness that reflected his ambivalent feelings toward her: on the one hand the desire for a physical conquest; and on the other a genuine eagerness to hurt her in some way.

"Yes," said Kathleen curtly, "here I am. I was hoping I'd be left alone for a change."

There was a toughness, she knew, in the fibre of Davy Dinsmore's make-up that made him immune to such remarks. The thoughts erupting from his brain penetrated to her at this close range, informing her that "this dame is pulling the same coy stuff. But I'll thaw her out yet."

A mind-curdling experience lay behind that calm conviction.

Kathleen closed her brain a little tighter to shut out the details of recollection that floated up from the complacent depths of the youth.

"I don't want you coming around me any more," Kathleen said with cold deliberation. "Your mind is like a sewer. I'm sorry I ever spoke to you when you first came ogling up to me. I should have known better, and I hope you realize I'm speaking to you plainly because otherwise you wouldn't believe I meant it. Well, I do—every word. Particularly the sewer part. Now, go away."

Davy's face had a bleached quality, but there was a rage in it and an intensity behind it that beat into her shielded mind. Instantly, she closed her brain still tighter, cutting off the vituperation that poured from him. It struck her abruptly that there was no fazing this creature unless she could absolutely humiliate him.

She snapped: "Beat it, you miserable, dough-fleshed thing!"

"Yaaah!" he said. And leaped for her.

For a second her surprise at his daring to pit himself against her superior strength held her stunned. Then, lips compressed, she grabbed at him, easily evading his flailing arms, and jerked him off his feet. Too late she realized that he had counted on her doing that. His rough fingers caught at her head, then clutched a handful of hair, and all the silk-thin tendrils that lay there in golden, glittering threads.

"O.K.," he exulted. "Now I've got you. *Don't let me down!* I know what you'd like to do. Get me down, grab my wrists, and squeeze till I let go. If you lower me as much as an inch, I'll give such a tug on those precious tendrils that some of them will tear loose. I know you can hold me up without getting tired—so hold!"

Dismay held Kathleen rigid. "Precious tendrils," he had said. So precious that for the first time in her life she had to throttle a scream. So precious that in some unthinking way she hadn't expected that anyone would dare to touch them. A half swoon of her fright closed over her like a night of wild and terrible storm.

"What do you want?" she gasped.

"Now you're talking," said Davy Dinsmore. But she didn't need his words. She had his mind now, flooding into her.

"All right," she said weakly, "I'll do it."

"And be sure to lower me slowly," the youth said. "And when my lips are touching yours, see that the kiss lasts at least a minute. I'll teach you to treat me like dirt."

His lips were swimming above hers against the hazy background of his sneering face and avid eyes, when a sharp, commanding voice rapped out in surprise and rage from behind her: "What's the meaning of this?"

"Huh!" stammered Davy Dinsmore. She felt his fingers leave

her hair and tendrils, then with a gasp she flung him down. He staggered, then caught himself and stammered: "I . . . I beg your pardon, Mr. Lorry. I . . . I—"

"Beat it, you miserable hound!" said Kathleen.

"Yes, go!" said Jem Lorry curtly.

Kathleen watched Davy go stumbling off, his mind sending out thoughts of pure fright at having offended one of the great men of the government. But when he disappeared, she did not turn to face the newcomer. Instinctively, she was aware of her muscles stiffening, as she kept her gaze and face averted from this man, the most powerful councillor in the cabinet of Kier Gray.

"And what was all that?" came the man's voice, not unpleasant, from behind her. "Apparently it was lucky I came up."

"Oh, I don't know," Kathleen replied coldly. She was in a mood for utmost candour. "Your attentions are equally repulsive to me."

"Hm-m-!" He came up beside her and she caught a glimpse of his strong jaw line, as he leaned over the railing.

"No difference, really," Kathleen said persistently. "You both want the same thing."

He stood silent for a moment, but his thoughts had the same elusive quality as Kier Gray's. The years had made him a master of evading her special powers of mind reading. When he finally spoke, his voice was changed. It held a harder quality. "No doubt your outlook on these matters will change after you become my mistress."

"That will be never!" snapped Kathleen. "I don't like human beings. I don't like you."

"Your objections are of no concern," the young man said coldly. "The only problem is how can I take possession of you without subjecting myself to the accusation that I am in secret alliance with the slans. Until I have thought of a solution to that, you may go your way."

His certainty sent a shudder through Kathleen. "You're quite mistaken," she said firmly. "The reason your intentions will inevitably fail is very simple. Kier Gray is my protector. Even you don't dare go against him."

Jem Lorry pondered that. Finally: "Your protector, yes. But he has no morals in the matter of a woman's virtue. I don't think he'll object if you become my mistress, but he will insist on my finding a propaganda-proof reason. He's become quite antislan these last few years. I used to think he was proslan. But now he's almost fanatic on the subject of having nothing to do with them. He and John Petty are closer on the subject now than they ever were. Funny!"

He mused on that for a moment; then: "But don't worry, I'll find a formula. I—"

A roar from a radio loud-speaker cut off Lorry's voice: "General warning! An unidentified aircraft was seen a few minutes ago, crossing the Rocky Mountains, headed eastward. Pursuing machines were rapidly outdistanced, and the ship seems to be taking a straight-line course toward Centropolis. People are ordered to go home immediately, as the ship—believed now to be of slan origin—will be here in one hour, according to present indications. The streets are needed for military purposes. Go home!"

The speaker clicked off; and Jem Lorry turned to Kathleen, a smile on his handsome face. "Don't let that arouse any hopes of rescue. One ship cannot carry important armaments, unless it has a mass of factories behind it. The old-style atomic bomb, for instance, could not possibly be manufactured in a cave, and besides, to be quite frank, the slans did not use it in the slan-human war. The disasters of that century, and earlier, were caused by slans, but not in that way."

He was silent for a minute, then: "Everybody thought those first bombs had solved the secret of atomic energy—" He stopped. Then: "It looks to me as if this trip was designed to give the more simple-minded human beings a scare, preliminary to an attempt to open negotiations."

An hour later, Kathleen stood beside Jem Lorry as the silver ship slanted toward the palace. Closer it came, travelling at enormous speed. Her mind reached out toward it, striving to contact the slans who must be inside.

The ship zoomed lower, nearer, but still there was no answering thought from the occupants. Suddenly a metallic capsule dropped from it. The capsule struck the garden path half a mile distant, and lay glinting like a jewel in the afternoon sun.

She looked up, and the ship was gone. No, there it was. Briefly she saw a silvery brilliance in the remote heights almost straight above the palace. It twinkled for a moment like a star. And was gone. Her straining eyes retreated from their violent effort; her mind came back from the sky; and she grew aware of Jem Lorry again. He exulted:

"Whatever else this means, it's what I've been waiting for—an opportunity to present an argument that will enable me to take you to my apartment this very night. There'll be a council meeting immediately, I imagine."

Kathleen drew a deep breath. She could see just how he might manage it, and the time had, therefore, come to fight with every weapon at her command. She spoke with dignity, her head flung back, her eyes flashing:

"I shall ask to be present at the council meeting on the grounds that I was in mental communication with the captain of the slans aboard the ship." She finished the lie calmly: "I can clarify certain things in the message that will be found in the capsule."

She thought desperately. Somehow she'd read in their minds what the message was, and from that she could build up a semi-reasonable story of what the slan leader had told her. If she was caught in the lie, there might be some dangerous reactions from these slan haters. But she had to prevent them from consenting to give her to Jem Lorry.

As she entered the council room, a conviction of defeat came to Kathleen. There were only seven men present, including Kier Gray. She stared at them one by one, reading as much of their minds as she could, and there was no help for her.

The four younger men were personal friends of Jem Lorry. The sixth man, John Petty, gave her one brief glance of icy hostility, then turned away indifferently.

Her gaze fastened finally on Kier Gray. A little anxious tremor of surprise whipped along her nerves, as she saw that he was staring at her with a laconic lifting of his eyebrows, and the faintest sneer on his lips. He caught her gaze and broke the silence.

"So you were in mental communication with the slan leader, were you?" He laughed harshly. "We'll let that pass for the moment."

There was so much incredulity in his voice and expression, so much hostility in his very attitude, that Kathleen was relieved when his cold eyes flicked away from her. He went on addressing the others:

"It's unfortunate that five councillors should be in the far corners of the world. I do not personally believe in roaming too far from headquarters; let subordinates do the travelling. However, we cannot delay discussion on a problem as urgent as this one. If the seven of us agree on a solution, we won't need their assistance. If we're deadlocked, we shall have to do a considerable amount of radio telephoning.

"Here is the gist of the contents of the metal capsule dropped by the slan ship. They claim that there are a million slans organized throughout the world—"

Jem Lorry interrupted sardonically, "Seems to me that our chief of secret police has been falling down on the job, despite his much-vaunted hatred of the slans."

Petty sat up and flashed him a cold glance. He snapped, "Perhaps you would exchange jobs with me for a year, and see what you can do. I wouldn't mind having the soft job of minister of state for a change."

Kier Gray's voice cut across the silence that followed Petty's freezing words. "Let me finish. They go on to say that not only does this organized million exist but there is, in addition, a vast total of unorganized men and women slans, estimated at ten millions more. What about that, Petty?"

"Undoubtedly there are some unorganized slans," the secret-police chief admitted cautiously. "We catch about a hundred a month all over the world, who have apparently never been part of any organization. In vast areas of the more primitive parts of the Earth, the people cannot be aroused to antipathy to slans; in fact, they accept them as human beings. And there are no doubt large colonies in some of these remote places, particularly in Asia, Africa, South America and Australia. It is years now since such colonies have actually been found, but we assume that some still exist, and that over the years they have developed self-protection to a high degree. I am prepared, however, to discount any activity from these remote sources. Civilization and science are built-up organisms, broadly based on the achievements, physical and mental, of hundreds of millions of beings. The moment these slans retreat to outlying sections of the Earth they defeat themselves, for they are cut off from books, and from that contact with civilized minds which is the only possible basis for a greater development.

"The danger is not, and never has been, from these remote slans but from those living in the big cities, where they are enabled to contact the greatest human minds and have, in spite of our precautions, some access to books. Obviously, this airship we saw today was built by slans who are living dangerously in the civilized centres."

Kier Gray nodded. "Much of what you surmise is probably true. But to get back to the letter, it goes on to say that these several million slans are only too anxious to end the period of strain which has existed between them and the human race. They denounce the ambition for world rule which actuated the first slans, explaining that ambition was due to a false conception of superiority, unleavened by the later experience that convinced them that they are not superior but merely different. They also accuse Samuel Lann, the human being and biological scientist who first created slans, and after whom slans are named—Samuel Lann: S. Lann: Slan—of fostering in his children the belief that they must rule the world. And that this belief, not any innate desire for domination, was the root of the disastrous ambitions of the early slans.

"Developing this idea, they go on to point out that the early inventions of the slans were simply minor improvements of already existing ideas. There has been, they claim, no really creative work done by the slans in physical science. They also state that their philosophers have come to the conclusion that the slans are not scientifically minded in any true sense of the word, differing from present-day human beings in that respect as widely as the ancient Greeks and Romans, who never developed science, as we know it, at all."

His words went on, but for a moment Kathleen heard with only half her mind. Could that be true? Slans not scientifically minded? Impossible. Science was simply an accumulation of facts, and the deduction of conclusions from those facts. And who better could bring divine order from intricate reality than the mighty-brained, full-grown, mature slan? She saw that Kier Gray was picking up a sheet of grey paper from his desk, and she brought her mind back to what he was saying.

"I'm going to read you the last page," he said in a colourless voice. " 'We cannot emphasize too strongly the importance of this. It means that slans can never seriously challenge the military might of human beings. Whatever improvements we may make on existing machinery and weapons will not decisively affect the outcome of a war, should such a disaster ever take place again.

" 'To our minds, there is nothing more futile than the present stalemate which, solving nothing, succeeds only in keeping the world in an unsettled condition and is gradually creating economic havoc from which human beings suffer to an ever-increasing degree.

" 'We offer peace with honour, the only basis of negotiation to be that slans must hereafter have the legal right to life, liberty and the pursuit of happiness.' "

Kier Gray laid the paper back on his desk, coldly flicked his gaze from face to face, and said in a flat, harsh voice:

"I'm absolutely against any compromise whatever. I used to think that something could be done, but no longer! Every slan out there"—he waved his hand significantly to cover half the globe—"must be exterminated."

The room, with its subdued lights and panelled walls, seemed dimmer to Kathleen, as if a shadow had fallen across her vision. In the silence even the pulsation of thoughts from the men was a quiet vibration in her brain, like the beat of waves on a remote, primeval shore. A whole world of shock separated her mind from the sense made by those thoughts—shock at the realization of the change that had taken place in Kier Gray.

Or was it change? Was it not possible that this man was as remorseless in his outlook as John Petty? His reason for keeping her alive must be exactly as he had said, for study purposes. And, of course, there was the time when he had believed, rightly or wrongly, that his political future was bound up in her continued existence. But nothing else. No feeling of compassion or pity, no interest in a helpless young creature for the sake of that creature. Nothing but the most materialistic outlook on life. This was the ruler of men whom she had admired, almost worshipped, for years. This was her protector!

It was true, of course, that the slans were lying. But what else could they do in dealing with people who knew only hate and lies? At least it was peace they offered, not war; and here was this man rejecting, without any consideration, an offer that would end four hundred or more years of criminal persecution of her race.

With a start, she grew aware that Kier Gray's eyes were fixed on her. His lips curled in sarcastic mirth as he said, "And now, let us hear the so-called message you received in your . . . er . . . mental communication with the slan commander."

Kathleen looked at him desperately. He didn't believe a word of her claim, and in the face of his scathing scepticism she knew better than to offer anything but the most carefully thought out statement to the mercilessly logical brain of this man. She needed time.

"I—" she began. "It was—"

She suddenly realized that Jem Lorry was on his feet. He was frowning. "Kier," he said, "that was pretty sharp tactics, offering your unqualified opposition to a matter as important as this, without giving the council a chance to discuss it. In view of your action, I am left no alternative but to state—with qualifications, however—that I am in favour of accepting this offer. My main qualification is this: the slans must agree to be assimilated into the human race. To that end, slans cannot marry each other, but must always marry human beings."

Kier Gray stared at him without hostility. "What makes you think there can be issue from a slan-human mating?"

"That's something I am going to find out," said Jem Lorry in a voice so casual that only Kathleen caught the intensity in it. She leaned forward, holding her breath. "I've decided to take Kathleen here as my mistress, and we shall see what we shall see. Nobody objects, I hope."

The younger men shrugged. Kathleen didn't need to read their minds to see that they hadn't the slightest objection. She noticed that John Petty was paying no attention to the conversation at all, and Kier Gray seemed lost in thought, as if he hadn't heard either.

With a gasp, she parted her lips to speak. Then shut them. A thought was suddenly in her brain. Suppose that intermarriage was the only solution to the slan problem. Suppose the council accepted Jem Lorry's solution! Even though she knew it to be based entirely on his passion for her, could she dare defend herself from him if there was the slightest possibility of those other slans out there agreeing to the plan, and thus ending hundreds of years of misery and murder?

She sank back in her chair, vaguely conscious of the irony of her position. She had come to the council chamber to fight for herself, and now she didn't dare utter a word. Kier Gray was speaking again:

"There is nothing new in this solution offered by Jem. Samuel Lann himself was intrigued by the possible result of such a mating and persuaded one of his granddaughters to marry a human being. No children were born of the union."

"I've got to prove that for myself!" said Jem Lorry doggedly. "This thing is too big to depend on one mating."

"There was more than one," Kier Gray said mildly.

Another man cut in impatiently: "The important thing is that assimilation does offer a solution, and there is no doubt that the human race will dominate the result. We're more than three and a half billion to, say, five million, which is probably a closer estimate than theirs. And even if no children can result, our ends are served in that, within two hundred years—figuring their normal life span at a hundred and fifty—there would be no slans alive."

It struck Kathleen with a shock that Jem Lorry had won his point. She saw in the vague, surface part of his mind that he had no intention of bringing the matter up again. Tonight he would send soldiers for her; and no one could say afterward that there had been any disagreement in the council. Their silence was consent.

For several minutes she was conscious only of a blur of voices, and of even more blurred thought. Finally, a phrase caught her mind. With an effort she turned her attention back to the men. The phrase "could exterminate them that way!" brought an electrifying awareness of how far they had gone from the original plan during those few minutes.

"Let us clarify this situation," said Kier Gray briskly. "The introduction of the idea of using some apparent agreement with the slans for exterminating them seems to have struck a responsive chord which—again—apparently seems to have eliminated from our various minds all thought of a true and honest agreement based on, for instance, the idea of assimilation.

"The schemes are, briefly, as follows. Number one: To allow them to intermingle with human beings until everyone has been thoroughly identified, then clamp down, catch most of them by surprise and track the others down within a short time.

"Plan number two: Force all slans to settle on an island, say Hawaii, and once we've got them there surround the place with battleships and planes and annihilate them.

"Plan number three: Treat them harshly from the beginning; insist on fingerprinting and photographing them, and on a plan for reporting to police at intervals, which will have both an element of strictness and fairness in it. This third idea may appeal to the slans because, if carried out over a period of time, it will seem to safeguard all except a small percentage which will be calling at police headquarters on any particular day. Its strictness will have the further psychological value of making them feel that we're being hard and careful, and will therefore, paradoxically, gradually ease their minds."

The cold voice went on, but somehow the whole scene lacked reality. They couldn't be sitting there discussing betrayal and murder on such a vast scale—seven men deciding for all the human race on a matter of more than life and death.

"What fools you are," Kathleen said bitingly. "Do you imagine for one minute that slans would be taken in by your silly schemes? Slans can read minds, and besides the whole thing is so transparent and ridiculous, every one of the schemes so open and barefaced, that I wonder how I could ever have thought any of you intelligent and clever."

They turned to stare at her silently, coldly. A faint, amused smile crinkled the lips of Kier Gray.

"I'm afraid you are at fault, not we. We assume that they are intelligent and suspicious, and therefore we do not offer any complicated idea; and that, of course, is the first element of successful propaganda. As for the reading of minds, we shall never meet the slan leaders. We shall transmit our majority opinion to the other five councillors, who will conduct negotiations under the firm conviction that we mean fair play. No subordinate will have any instructions except that the matter is to be fairly conducted. So you see—"

"Just a minute," said John Petty, and there was so much satisfaction in his voice, such an exultant ring, that Kathleen turned toward him with a start. "Our main danger is not from ourselves but from the fact that this slan girl has overheard our plans. She has said that she was in mental communication with the commander of the slans on board the ship which approached the palace. In other words, they now know she is here. Suppose another ship comes near; she would then be in a position to inform our enemies of our plans. Naturally, she must be killed at once."

A mind-shattering dismay burned through Kathleen. The logic of the argument could not be gainsaid. She saw the gathering realization of it in the minds of the men. By trying so desperately to escape the attentions of Jem Lorry, she had walked into a trap that could end only in death.

Kathleen's gaze continued in fascination upon John Petty's face. The man was aglow with a deep-rooted pleasure that he could not hide. There was no doubt that he had not expected such a victory. Surprise made the thrill all the greater.

It was with reluctance that she turned from him and concentrated on the other men. The vague thoughts that had already come from them came now in a more concentrated form from each in turn. And there was no doubt about what they thought. Their decision gave no particular pleasure to the younger men who, unlike Jem Lorry, had no personal interest in her. But their conviction was an unalterable thing. Death.

It seemed to Kathleen that the finality of the verdict was written in the face of Jem Lorry. The man's manner, as he turned on her, showed his dismay.

"You damned little fool!" he said.

With that he started to chew viciously on his lower lip, and sank back in his chair, staring moodily at the floor.

She was dazed now. She stared for a long moment at Kier Gray before she even saw him. With horror she watched the startled frown that creased his forehead, the unconcealed, thunderstruck expression in his eyes. That gave her an instant of courage. He didn't want her dead, or he wouldn't be so alarmed.

The courage, and the hope that came with it, vanished like a star behind a black cloud. His very dismay showed that he had no solution to the problem that had dropped into the room like a bombshell. Slowly, his expression changed to impassivity, but she felt no hope until he said:

"Death would perhaps be the necessary solution if it were true that she was in communication with a slan aboard that ship. Fortunately for her, she was telling a lie. There were no slans on the plane. The ship was robot-propelled."

A man said, "I thought robot-propelled ships could be captured by radio interference with their mechanism."

"So they can," said Kier Gray. "You may remember how the slan ship darted straight upward when it disappeared. The slan controllers shot it off like that when they suddenly realized we were tampering successfully with their ship."

The leader smiled grimly. "We fought the ship down into the swampland a hundred miles south of here. It was pretty badly wrecked, from all reports, and they haven't got it out yet; but it will be taken in due course to the great Cudgen machine works, where, no doubt, its mechanism will be analysed." He added, "The reason it took so long was that the robot mechanism was on a slightly different principle, requiring a new combination of radio waves to dominate it."

"All that is unimportant," John Petty said impatiently. "What counts is that this slan has been here in the room, has heard our plans to annihilate her people, and may therefore be dangerous to us in that she will do her best to inform other slans of what we contemplate. She must be killed."

66

Kier Gray stood up slowly, and the face he turned to John Petty was grim. His voice, when he spoke, held a metallic note. "I have told you, sir, that I am making a sociological study of this slan, and I will thank you to refrain from further attempts to execute her. You have said some hundred slans are caught and executed every month, and the slans claim that some eleven million others still exist. I hope"—and his voice was edged with sarcasm—"I hope I shall be permitted the privilege of keeping alive one slan for scientific purposes, one slan whom, apparently, you hate more than all the others put together—"

John Petty cut in sharply, "That's all very well, Kier. What I'd like to know is, why did Kathleen Layton lie about being in communication with the slans?"

Kathleen drew a deep breath. The chill of those few minutes of deadly danger was oozing out of her, but there was still a choked-up sensation of emotion. She said shakily, "Because I knew Jem Lorry was going to try to make me his mistress, and I wanted you to know that I objected."

She felt the tremor of thoughts that swept out from the men, and saw their facial expressions: understanding, then impatience.

"For heaven's sake, Jem," one exclaimed, "can't you keep your love affairs out of our council meetings?"

Another said, "With all due respect to Kier Gray, there is something intolerable about a slan objecting to anything that a human being with authority may plan for her. I am curious to see what the issue would be from such a mating. Your objections are overruled; and now, Jem, have your guard take her up to your apartment. And I hope that ends this discussion!"

For the first time in her seventeen years, it struck Kathleen that there was a limit to the nervous tension that a slan could endure. There was a tautness inside her, as if somewhere something vital was at the breaking point. She was conscious of no thought of her own. She just sat there, painfully gripping the plastic smoothness of the arms of her chair. Abruptly, she grew aware of a thought inside her brain, a sharp, lashing thought from Kier Gray.

"You little fool! How did you get yourself into this mess?"

She looked at him then, miserably, seeing for the first time that he was leaning back in his chair, eyes half closed, lips drawn tight. He said finally:

"All this would be very well if such matings needed testing. They don't. Case histories of more than a hundred slan-human attempts to reproduce children are available in the file library under the heading 'Abnormal Marriages'.

"The reasons for the sterility are difficult to define because men and slans do not appear to differ from each other to any marked degree. The amazingly tough musculature of the slan is due, not to a new type of muscle, but to a speeding up of the electro-explosions that actuate the muscles. There is also an increase in the number of nerves to every part of the body, making it tremendously more sensitive.

"The two hearts are not really two hearts, but a combination, each section of which can operate independent of the other. Nor are the two together very much larger than the one original. They're simply finer pumps.

"Again, the tendrils that send and receive thoughts are growths from formerly little-known formations at the top of the brain, which, obviously, must have been the source of all the vague mental telepathy known to earlier human beings and still practised by people everywhere.

"So you see that what Samuel Lann did with his mutation machine to his wife, who bore him the first three slan babies— one boy and two girls—over six hundred years ago, has not added anything new to the human body, but changed or mutated what already existed."

It seemed to Kathleen that he was talking to gain time. In that one brief mental flash from him, there had been overtones of a complete understanding of the situation. He must know that no amount of reasonable argument could dissuade the passions of a man like Jem Lorry. She heard his voice go on.

"I am giving you this information because apparently none of you has ever bothered to investigate the true situation as compared to popular beliefs. Take, for instance, the so-called superior intelligence of the slan, referred to in the letter received from them today. There is an old illustration on that point which has been buried by the years; an experiment in which Samuel Lann, that extraordinary man, brought up a monkey baby, a human baby and a slan baby under rigidly scientific conditions. The monkey was the most precocious, learning within a few months what the slan and the human baby required considerably longer to assimilate. Then the human and slan learned to talk, and the monkey was hopelessly outdistanced. The slan and the human continued at a fairly even pace until, at the age of four, the slan's powers of mental telepathy began painfully to operate. At this point, the slan baby forged into the lead.

"However, Dr. Lann later discovered that by intensification of the human baby's education, it was possible for the latter to catch up to, and remain reasonably level with, the slan, particularly in quickness of mind. The slan's great advantage was the ability to read minds, which gave him an unsurpassable insight into psychology and readier access to the education which the human child could grasp only through the medium of ears and eyes—"

John Petty interrupted in a voice that was thick and harsh:

"What you're saying is only what I've known all along, and is the main reason why we can't begin to consider peace negotiations with these . . . these damned artificial beings. In order for a human being to equal a slan, he must strain for years to acquire what comes with the greatest of ease to the slan. In other words, all except the minutest fraction of humanity is incapable of ever being anything more than a slave in comparison to a slan. Gentlemen, there can be no peace, but rather an intensification of extermination methods. We can't risk one of the Machiavellian plans already discussed, because the danger of something going wrong is too great."

A councillor said, "He's right!"

Several voices echoed the conviction; and there was suddenly no doubt which way the verdict would go. Kathleen saw Kier Gray glance keenly from face to face. He said:

"If that is to be our decision, then I should consider it a grave mistake for any one of us at the present time to take this slan as mistress. It might give a wrong impression."

The silence that followed was the silence of agreement, and Kathleen's gaze leaped to Jem Lorry's face. He met her eyes coolly, rising languidly to his feet as she stood up and made for the door. As she passed he fell into step at her side.

He opened the door for her and spoke in a low voice. "It won't be for long, my lady. So don't build up false hopes." And he smiled confidently.

But it was not of his threat that Kathleen was thinking as she walked slowly along the corridor. She was remembering the thunderstruck expression that had come into Kier Gray's face at the moment John Petty had asked for her death.

It didn't fit. It didn't fit at all with his suave words of a minute later, when he had informed the others that the slan ship was robot-propelled and had been brought down in the marshes. If that were so, then why had he been startled? And if it weren't so, then Kier Gray had taken the terrible risk of lying for her and was probably even now worrying about it.

9

Jommy Cross stared urgently yet thoughtfully down at the human wreck that was Granny. There was no rage in him at her betrayal of him. The result was disaster, his future abruptly blank, unplanned, homeless.

His first problem was what to do with the old woman.

She sat blithely in a chair, an extravagantly rich and colourful dressing gown swaddled jauntily around her ungainly form. She giggled up at him. "Granny knows something, yes, Granny knows—" Her words trailed into nonsense, then, "Money, oh, good Lord, yes. Granny's got plenty of money for her old age. See!"

With the trusting innocence of a drink-sodden old soak, she slid a bulging black bag from inside her dressing gown, then with ostrichlike common sense jerked it back into hiding.

Jommy Cross was conscious of shock. It was the first time he had actually seen her money, although he had always known her various hiding places. But to have the stuff out here now, with a raid actually in progress—such stupidity deserved the furthest limits of punishment.

But still he stood undecided, becoming tenser as the first faint pressure of men's thoughts from outside the shack made an almost impalpable weight against his brain. Dozens of men, edging closer, the snub noses of their submachine guns protruding ahead of them. He frowned blackly. By all rights, he should leave the betrayer to face the rage of the baffled hunters, to face the law which said that every human being, without exception, who was convicted of harbouring a slan must be hanged by the neck until dead.

Through his mind ran the nightmare picture of Granny on the way to the gallows, Granny shrieking for mercy, Granny fighting to prevent the rope from being placed around her neck, kicking, scratching, slobbering at her captors.

He reached down and grabbed her naked shoulders where the dressing gown was loosely drawn. He shook her with a cold, deadly violence until her teeth rattled, until she sobbed with a dry, horrible pain, and a modicum of sanity came into her eyes. He said harshly:

"It's death for you if you stay here. Don't you know the law?"

"Huh!" She sat up, briefly startled, then abruptly slipped off again into the cesspool of her mind.

70

Hurry, hurry, he thought, and forced his brain into that squalor of thought to see if his words had brought any basic balance. Just as he was about to give up he found a startled, dismayed, alert little section of sanity almost buried in the dissolving, incoherent mass that was her thoughts.

" 'S all right," she mumbled. "Granny's got plenty of money. Rich people don't get hung. Stands to reason."

Jommy stepped back from her, indecisive. The weight of the men's minds was a heavy, dragging thing on his brain. They were drawing ever nearer, drawing an ever-tighter circle. Their number appalled him. Even the great weapon in his pocket might be useless if a hail of bullets swept the flimsy walls of the shack. And only one bullet was needed to destroy all his father's dreams.

"By God," he said aloud. "I'm a fool! What will I do with you even if I get you out? All highways out of the city will be blocked. There's only one real hope, and that will be almost hopelessly difficult even without a drunken old woman to hinder me. I don't fancy climbing a thirty-storey building with you on my back."

Logic said he should abandon her. He half turned away; and then, once more, the thought of Granny being hanged came in all its horror. Whatever her faults, her very existence had made it possible for him to remain alive. That was a debt which must be paid. With a single snatching movement he tore the black bag from its hiding place under Granny's dressing gown. She grunted drunkenly, and then awareness seeped into her as he held the bag tantalizingly before her eyes.

"Look," he taunted, "all your money, your whole future. You'll starve. They'll have you scrubbing floors in the poorhouse. They'll whip you."

In fifteen seconds she was sober, a hot, burning soberness that grasped essentials with all the clarity of the hardened criminal.

"Granny'll hang!" she gasped.

"Now we're getting somewhere," Jommy Cross said. "Here, take your money." He smiled grimly as she grabbed it from him. "We've got a tunnel to go through. It leads from my bedroom to a private garage at the corner of 470th street. I've got a key to the car. We'll drive down near the Air Centre and steal one of—"

He stopped, conscious of the flimsiness of that final part of his plan. It seemed incredible that the tendrilless slans would be so poorly organized that he would actually be able to get one of those marvellous spaceships which they launched nightly into the sky. True, he had escaped from them once with absurd ease, but . . .

With a gasp, Jommy set the old woman down on the flat roof of the spaceship building. He collapsed beside her heavily and lay there panting. For the first time in his life he was conscious of muscular weariness contracted from exertion at the full of vibrant health.

"Good heaven," he breathed, "who'd have thought an old woman would weigh so much?"

She was snarling in retrospective terror from that frightful climb. His brain caught the first warning of the burst of vituperation that was rising to her lips. His weary muscles galvanized instantly. One swift hand clamped over her mouth.

"Shut up," he said, "or I'll drop you over the edge like a sack of potatoes. You're the cause of this situation, and you've got to bear the consequences."

His words acted like cold water. He had to admire the way she recuperated from the terror that had racked her. The old creature certainly had staying powers. She pulled his hand from her mouth and asked sullenly, "What now?"

"We've got to find a way into the building in as short a time as possible and—" He glanced at his wrist watch and, dismayed, leaped to his feet. Twelve minutes of ten! Twelve minutes before the rocketship took off. Twelve minutes to take control of that ship!

He snatched Granny up, flung her lightly over his shoulder and raced off toward the centre of the roof. Not only was there no time to search for doors but such doors would obviously be wired, and there was even less time to study and nullify the alarm system. There was only one way. Somewhere there must be the runway up which the ships were projected when they were launched toward the remote regions of interplanetary space.

He felt the difference beneath his feet, a vague rise, a gentle bulbousness. He stopped short, teetering on his toes, unbalanced by the violent ending of his racing flight. Carefully, he felt his way back to the beginning of the bulbous section. That would be the edge of the runway. Swiftly, he tore his father's atomic gun from his pocket. Its disintegrating fire flamed downward.

He peered through the four-foot-diameter hole into a tunnel that sloped to depths at an angle that must have been a tight sixty degrees. A hundred, two hundred, three hundred yards of glittering metallic wall, and then the ship gradually took on outline as Jommy's eyes grew accustomed to the dim light. He saw a torpedo-pointed nose, with forward blast tubes distorting the smooth, streamlined effect. It seemed a deadly thing, silent and motionless now, yet menacing.

He had the illusion of staring down the barrel of a vast gun, at the shell that was about to be fired. The comparison struck him so sharply that for a long moment his mind refused to hold the thought of what he must do. Doubt came. Did he dare slide

72

down that glass-smooth slipway when any second a rocketship would come smashing up toward the sky?

His body felt cold. With an effort, he lifted his gaze from the paralysing depth of tunnel and fixed his eyes, at first unseeing, then with gathering fascination, on the distant, looming splendour of the palace. His thought paused abruptly; slowly his body lost its tension. For long seconds he just stood there, drinking in the glory of the immense, exquisite jewel that was the palace by night.

It was plainly visible from this height between and beyond two great skyscrapers; and it glowed brilliantly. There was no mind-staggering, eye-dazzling glare to it. It glowed with a soft, living, wonderful flame that was never the same colour for more than an instant: glorious, lambent fire that flickered and flashed a thousand combinations, and each combination was subtly, sometimes startlingly, different. Not once was there an exact repetition.

On and on it sparkled, and *lived*! Once, for a long moment, chance turned the tower, that translucent five-hundred-foot fairy tower, a glowing turquoise blue. And for that instant the visible part of the palace below was nearly all a deeply glowing ruby red. For one moment—and then the combination shattered into a million bursting fragments of colour: blue, red, green, yellow. No colour, no possible shade of colour, was missing from that silent, flaming explosion.

A thousand nights he had fed his soul on its beauty, and now he felt again the wonder of it. Strength poured from it into him. His courage came back like the unbreakable, indestructible force it was. His teeth clenched, grimly he stared down into the depths so sharply angled, so smooth in the promise of madly swift passage to the distant, steel-hard bottom.

The danger of it was like a symbol of his future. Blank future, less predictable now than it had ever been. It was only good sense to believe that the tendrilless slans were aware that he was here on this roof. There must be alarm systems—there *must* be.

"What do you keep staring down that hole for?" Granny whined. "Where's the door we want? Time is—"

"Time!" said Jommy Cross. His watch said four minutes to ten, and that seemed to shock every nerve in his body. Eight minutes actually gone, *four* minutes left in which to conquer a fortress. He caught Granny's thought then, her abrupt awareness of his intention. Just in time his hand slapped at her mouth, and her shriek of dismay was stifled against his palm. The next second they were falling, committed irrevocably.

They struck the tunnel surface almost gently, as if they had suddenly entered a world of slow motion. The slipway felt, not hard, but yielding beneath his body, and there was only the vaguest sense of motion. But his eyes and mind were not fooled.

73

The blunt nose of the spaceship plunged up at them. The illusion of the ship roaring toward them in full blast was so real that he had to fight a wild impulse to panic.

"Quick!" he hissed at Granny. "Use the flat of your hands— *slow down!*"

The old woman needed no urging. Of all the instincts in her misused body that of survival was strongest. She couldn't have screamed now to save her soul, but her lips blubbered with fear even as she fought for life. Her bead-like eyes glistened with a moist terror—but she fought! She clung at the gleaming metal, bony hands spread out flat and hard, her legs squeezed against the metal surface; and pitiful though the result was, it helped.

Abruptly, the nose of the ship loomed above Jommy Cross, higher than he had expected. With a desperate strength, he reached up at the first thick ring of rocket chambers. His fingers touched the corded, seared metal, skidded—and instantly lost their hold.

He fell back, and only then did he realize that he had risen to the full stretched-out height of his body. He fell hard, almost stunningly, but instantly, with the special strength of slan muscles, he was up again. His fingers caught one of the big tubes of the second ring of fire chambers with such unbreakable hold that the uncontrollable part of the journey ended. Sick from the strain of overeffort, he let go, and it was as he half sat there shaking the dizziness out of his head that he grew aware of the patch of light farther under the immense body of the machine.

The ship was curving so sharply now toward the tunnel floor on which it rested that he had to bend double as he made his way painfully toward it. He was thinking: An open door, here, now, a few short seconds before the great ship is due to leave. It is a door! An opening, two feet in diameter, in a foot-thick metal hull, with the hinged door leaning inward. He pushed up into the opening unhesitatingly, his terrible gun alert for the slightest movement. But there was no one.

In that first glance he saw that this was the control room. There were some chairs, an intricate-looking instrument board, and some great, curved, glowing plates on either side of it. And there was an open door leading to the second section of the ship. It took but a moment to leap inside and pull the panicky old woman after him. And then, lightly, he jumped for the connecting door.

At the threshold he paused cautiously and peered in. This second room was partly furnished with chairs, the same deep, comfortable chairs as were in the control room. But more than half the space was filled with chained-down packing cases. There were two doors. One led to what was obviously a third section of the long ship. It was partly open, with more packing cases

74

visible beyond and, vaguely, a door leading into a fourth compartment. But it was the second door in the second room that made Jommy Cross freeze motionless where he was.

It was on the side beyond the chairs and led outside. A blaze of light poured from the great room there into the ship, and there were figures of men. He opened his mind wide. Instantly a thought wash from many brains came to him, so many of them that the combined leakage from behind their defective shields brought dozens of half thoughts, menacingly alert thoughts, as if scores of tendrilless slans out there were waiting for something.

He cut the thought off, whirled toward the instrument board that dominated the whole front part of the control room. The board itself was about a yard wide, two yards long, a metal-mounted bank of glowing tubes and shining mechanisms. There were more than a dozen control levers of various kinds, all within reach of the finely built chair facing them.

On either side of the instrument board were the great, curved, glossy, semimetallic plates he had already noticed. The concave surface of each towering section glowed with a subdued light of its own. It would be impossible to solve the alien control system in the few moments at his disposal. Tight-lipped, he sprang forward into the control chair. With swift, deliberately crude purpose, he activated every switch and lever on the panel.

A door clanged metallically. There was an abrupt, wonderful sense of lightness; swift, almost body-crushing forward movement, and then a faint, throbbing bass roar. Instantly the purpose of the great curved plates became apparent. On the one to the right appeared a picture of the sky ahead. Jommy could see lights and land far below, but the ship was mounting too steeply for the Earth to be more than a distortion at the bottom of the plate.

It was the left visiplate that showed the glory, a picture of a city of lights, so vast that it staggered the imagination, falling away behind the ship. Far to one side he caught the night splendour of the palace.

And then the city was gone into distance behind them. Carefully, he shut off the mechanisms he had actuated, watching for the effect of each in turn. In two minutes the complicated board was solved and the simple machinery under control. The purpose of four of the switches was not clear, but that could wait.

He levelled off, for it was no part of his intention to go out into airless space. That demanded intimate knowledge of every screw and plate in the machine, and his first purpose must be to establish a new, safe base of operations. Then, with his ship to take him where he willed to go . . .

His brain soared. There was in him suddenly an extravagant sense of power. A thousand things remained to be done, but at last he was out of his cage, old enough and strong enough, mentally and physically, to live a secure, defensive existence. There were years to be passed, long years that separated him from maturity. All his father's science must be learned, and used. Above all, his first real plan for finding the true slans must be carefully thought out and the first exploratory moves made.

The thought ended as he grew abruptly aware of Granny. The old woman's thought had been a gentle beat against his mind all these minutes. He was aware of her going into the next room, and deep in his mind was a developing picture of what she was seeing. And now—just like that—the picture went dead slow, as if she had suddenly closed her eyes.

Jommy Cross snatched his gun and simultaneously whirled and leaped to one side. There was a flash of fire from the doorway that seared across the place where his head had been. The flame touched the instrument board, then winked out. The tall, fullgrown, tendrilless slan woman standing in the doorway whipped the muzzle of her little silver gun toward him—then her whole body went rigid as she saw his weapon pointing at her. They stood like that for a long, frozen moment. The woman's eyes became glittering pools.

"You damned snake!"

In spite of anger, almost because of it, her voice was golden in its vibrant beauty, and abruptly Jommy Cross felt beaten. The sight of her and the sound of her brought sudden poignant memory of his glorious mother, and he knew with a sense of helplessness that he could no more blast this marvellous creature out of existence than he could have destroyed his own mother. In spite of his mighty gun threatening her as her weapon threatened him, he was actually at her mercy. And the way she had fired at his back showed the hot determination that burned behind those gleaming grey eyes. Murder! The mad hatred of the tendrilless slan against the true slan.

Dismayed though he was, Jommy studied her with growing fascination. Slimly, strongly, lithely built, she stood there, poised, alert, leaning forward on one foot a little breathlessly, like a runner tense for the race. Her right hand, holding the weapon, was a slender, finely shaped thing, beautifully tanned and supple-looking. Her left hand was half hidden behind her back, as if she had been walking briskly along, arms swinging freely, and then had frozen in mid-stride, one arm up and one swung back.

Her dress was a simple tunic, drawn in snugly at her waist; and what a proudly tilted head she had, hair gleaming dark brown, bobbed and curled. Her face, below that crown, was the epitome of sensitive loveliness, lips not too full, nose lean and shapely, cheeks delicately moulded. Yet it was the subtle shaping of her cheeks that gave her face the power, the sheer intellectual

76

forcefulness. Her skin looked soft and clear, the purest of unblemished complexions, and the grey of her eyes was darkly luminous.

No, he couldn't shoot; he couldn't blast this exquisitely beautiful woman out of existence. And yet—yet he must make her think that he could. He stood there, watching the surface of her mind, the little half thoughts that flicked across it. There was in her shield the same quality of incomplete coverage that he had already noticed in the tendrilless slans, due probably to their inability to read minds and therefore to realize what complete coverage actually meant.

For the moment he could not allow himself to follow the little memory vibrations that pulsed from her. All that counted was that he was standing here facing this tremendously dangerous woman, his weapon and her weapon levelled, every nerve and muscle in their two bodies pitched to the ultimate key of alertness.

The woman spoke first. "This is very foolish," she said. "We should sit down, put our weapons on the floor in front of us and talk this thing over. That would relieve the intolerable strain, but our positions would remain materially the same."

Jommy Cross felt startled. The suggestion showed a weakness in the face of danger that was not indicated anywhere in that highly courageous head and face. The fact that she had made it added instantly to the psychological strength of his position, but he was conscious of suspicion, a conviction that her offer must be examined for special dangers. He said slowly, "The advantage would be yours. You're a grown-up slan, your muscles are better co-ordinated. You could reach your gun faster than I could reach mine."

She nodded matter-of-factly. "That's true. But actually you have the advantage in your ability to watch at least part of my mind."

"On the contrary"—he spoke the lie smoothly—"when your mind shield is up the coverage is so complete that I could not possibly divine your purpose before it was too late."

The uttering of the words brought him awareness of how incomplete her coverage really was. In spite of his having kept his mind concentrated on danger and out of the trickling stream of her thought, enough had come through to give him a brief but coherent history of the woman.

Her name was Joanna Hillory. She was a regular pilot on the Martian Way, but this was to be her last trip for many months. The reason was that she had recently married an engineer stationed on Mars, and now she was going to have a baby—so she was being assigned to duties that put less strain on her system than the constant pressure of acceleration to which she was subjected in space travel.

Jommy Cross began to feel easier. A newlywed expecting a child was not likely to take desperate chances. He said, "Very well, let us put our guns down simultaneously and sit down."

When the guns were on the floor, Jommy Cross glanced across at the slan woman, puzzled by the faintly amused smile that twisted her lips. The smile became broader, more distinctly ironic. "And now that you have disarmed yourself," she said softly, "you will prepare to die!"

In utter dismay, Jommy Cross stared at the tiny gun that glittered in her left hand. She must have held the toy-sized weapon concealed there all those tense moments, awaiting with a mocking certainty the opportunity of using it. Her golden-rich voice, beautiful as music, went on:

"So you swallowed all that about my being a poor little bride, with a baby coming and an anxious husband waiting! A full-grown snake wouldn't have been so credulous. As it is, the young snake I'm looking at will die for his incredible stupidity."

10

JOMMY CROSS stared at the little gun held so firmly, so un-waveringly by the tendrilless slan woman. Through his shock and dismay he became suddenly aware of a background to his chagrin, the smooth-flowing enormously swift movement of the ship. There was no acceleration, simply that tireless, hurtling pace, the mile on mile of headlong flight with no indication whether they were still in Earth's atmosphere or in free space.

He stood there dismayed. His mind was free of terror, but it was also totally empty of any plan. All thought of action had been driven from his mind for the moment by the startling realization that he had been completely outwitted. The woman had used her very defects to defeat him.

She must have known her thought shield was faulty, and so, with almost animal cunning, she had allowed that pathetic little story to leak through, designed to show him that she would never, oh, never, have the courage for a fight to the finish. It was easy to see now that her courage was a chilled-steel quality that he could not hope to equal for years.

He moved obediently to one side as she gestured menacingly, and then watched her alertly as she bent to pick up the two weapons on the floor, first her own, then his. But not for the barest instant did her eyes shift from him, and there was not a quiver of weakness in the way her gun pointed at him.

She put away the small weapon that had tricked him, kept her larger gun in her right hand, and, without a glance at his gun, locked it in a drawer beneath the glowing instrument board.

Her alertness left no hope that he might trick her into turning her weapon aside. The fact that she had not shot him immediately must mean that she wanted to talk to him first. But he could not leave that possibility to chance. He said huskily:

"Do you mind if I ask a few questions before you kill me?"

"I'll ask the questions," she replied coolly. "There can be no purpose in your satisfying any curiosity you may have. How old are you?"

"Fifteen."

She nodded. "Then you are at a stage of mental and emotional development where you will appreciate even a few minutes' reprieve from death; and, like an adult human being, you will probably be pleased to know that so long as you answer my questions I will not pull the trigger of this electric-energy gun, though the final result will be death just the same."

Jommy Cross wasted no time in even thinking about her words. He said, "How do you know I'll tell the truth?"

Her smile was confident. "Truth is implicit in the cleverest lies. We tendrilless slans, lacking the ability to read minds, have been forced by necessity to develop psychology to the utmost limits. But never mind that. Were you sent to steal this ship?"

"No."

"Then who are you?"

Quietly he gave her a brief history of his life. As his story developed, he grew conscious that the woman's eyes were narrowing, lines of surprise gathering on her forehead.

"Are you trying to tell me," she cut in sharply, "that you are the little boy who came into the main offices of Air Centre six years ago?"

He nodded. "It was a shock to find a crew so murderous that even a child must be destroyed forthwith. It—"

He stopped because the woman's eyes were aflame. "So it's come at last," she said slowly. "For six long years we've discussed and analysed, uncertain whether we were right in letting you escape."

"You . . . let . . . me . . . escape!" gasped Jommy Cross.

She ignored him, went on as if she hadn't heard. "And ever since we've waited anxiously for a follow-up from the snakes. We were pretty sure they wouldn't betray us because they wouldn't want our greatest invention, the spaceship, to fall into the hands of human beings. The main question in our minds was, what was behind that first exploratory manoeuvre? Now, in your attempted theft of a rocketship, we have the answer."

Startled into silence, Jommy Cross listened to the mistaken analysis. Dismay grew in him. Dismay that had nothing to do with his personal danger. It was the incredible insanity of this slan-versus-slan war. The deadliness of it was almost beyond imagination. Joanna Hillory went on in her vibrant voice, tinged now with triumph.

"It's good to know for sure what we have so long suspected, and the evidence is almost overwhelming now. We have explored the Moon, Mars and Venus. We have gone as far afield as the moons of Jupiter, and not once have we seen an alien spaceship or the faintest sign of a snake.

"The conclusion is inescapable. For some reason, perhaps because their revealing tendrils make it necessary for them to be ever on the move, they have never developed the antigravity screens that make the rocketship possible. Whatever the reason, the chain of logic points inexorably to the fact that they do lack space travel."

"You and your logic," said Jommy Cross, "are beginning to be very tiresome. It seems unbelievable that a slan could be so wrong. For just one second, take a reasonable attitude and assume, just assume, that my story is true."

She smiled, a thin smile that barely touched her lips. "From the beginning, there were only two possibilities. The first one I have already outlined. The other—that you actually have had no contact with slans—has worried us for years.

"You see, if you were sent by the slans, then they already knew we controlled Airways. But if you were an independent slan, then you had a secret that sooner or later, when you did contact the snakes, would be dangerous to us. In short, if your story is true, we must kill you to prevent you at some future date from apprising them of our special knowledge, and because it is our policy to take no chances whatsoever with snakes. In any case, you are as good as dead."

Her words were harsh, her tone icy. But far more menacing than her tone, Jommy realized, was the fact that neither right nor wrong, truth nor untruth, mattered to this slan woman. His world was shattering before the thought that if this immorality was slan justice, then slans had nothing to offer the world that could begin to match the sympathy, kindliness and pervading gentleness of spirit that he had seen so often in the minds of the lowly human beings. If all adult slans were like this, then there was no hope.

His mind hovered over the fearful, dizzying gulf of the senseless feud between slan, human being and tendrilless slan, and a thought more dark and terrible than night swept him. Was it really possible that his father's great dreams and greater works were to be blotted out in a solitary waste of nothingness, destroyed and ruined by these insane fratricides? The papers of his father's secret science, which he had removed from the catacombs such a short time before, were in his pockets; they would be used and abused by the cruel, merciless tendrilless slans if this woman carried out her desire to kill him. In spite of logic, in spite of the certainty that he could not hope to catch a full-grown slan off guard, he must stay alive in order to prevent that from happening.

His gaze narrowed on her face, conscious of the shadowy lines of thought in her forehead, a thoughtfulness that yet did not interfere with her alertness. The lines smoothed as she said:

"I have been considering your special case. I have, of course, authority to destroy you without consulting our council. The question is, does the problem you present merit their attention? Or will a brief report be sufficient? It is not a question of mercy, so allow yourself no hope."

But hope did come. It would take time to take him before the council, and time was life. He said urgently, yet conscious of the need for calm words, "I must admit my own reason is paralysed by the feud between slan and tendrilless slan. Don't your people realize how tremendously the entire slan position would improve if you would co-operate with the 'snakes', as you call them? Snakes! The very word is a proof of intellectual bankruptcy, suggestive of a propaganda campaign, replete with slogans and emotion words."

The grey fire came back into her eyes, but there was scathing mockery in her voice: "A little history may enlighten you on the matter of slan co-operation. For nearly four hundred years there have been tendrilless slans. Like the true slans, they're a distinct race, being born without tendrils, which is the only differentiation from the snakes. For security's sake, they formed communities in remote districts where the danger of discovery was reduced to a minimum. They were prepared to be completely friendly with the true slans against the common enemy—human beings!

"What was their horror, then, to find themselves attacked and murdered, their carefully built up, isolated civilization destroyed by fire and weapon—by the true slans! They made desperate efforts to establish contact, to become friends, but it was useless. They finally discovered that only in the highly dangerous, human-controlled cities could they find any safety. There the true slans, because of their revealing tendrils, dared not venture.

"Snakes!" The mockery was gone from her voice. Only a hard bitterness remained. "What other word can possibly fit? We don't hate them, but we have a sense of utter frustration and distrust. Our policy of destroying them is pure self-defence, but it has become a ruthless, unyielding attitude."

"But surely your leaders could talk things over with them?"

"Talk things over with whom? In the last three hundred years we have never located a single hiding place of the true slan. We've captured some that attacked us. We've killed a few in running fights. But we've never discovered anything about them. They exist, but where and how and what their purpose is we haven't the faintest idea. There is no greater mystery on the face of the Earth."

Jommy Cross interrupted tensely: "If this is true, if you're not lying, please, madam, let your shield down for a moment so that I can be sure that your words are true! I, too, have thought this feud insane ever since I first discovered that there were two kinds of slans, and that they were at war. If I could become absolutely convinced that the madness is one-sided, why, I could—"

Her voice, sharp as a slap in the face, cut across his words. "What would you do? Help us? Are you under the impression that we would ever believe such an intention, and allow you to go free? The more you talk, the more dangerous I consider you. We have always made the assumption that a snake, by reason of his ability to read minds, is our superior, and therefore must not be given time to effect an escape. Your youth has saved you for ten minutes, but now that I know your story I can see no purpose in keeping you alive. Furthermore, there seems no reason why your case should be brought before the council. One more question—then you die!"

Jommy Cross stared angrily at the woman. There was no friendliness in him now, no sense of any kinship between this woman and his mother. If she were telling the truth, then it was the tendrilless slans he should sympathize with, not the mysterious, elusive true slans who were acting with such incomprehensible ruthlessness. But sympathy or no, every word she had spoken showed more clearly how dangerous it would be to allow the mightiest weapon the world would ever know to fall into this seething hell's brew of hatred. He must defeat this woman, must save himself. *Must.* He said swiftly:

"Before you ask that last question, consider seriously what an unprecedented opportunity has come to you. Is it possible that you are going to allow hatred to distort your reason? According to your statement, for the first time in the history of tendrilless slans you have caught a tendrilled slan who is absolutely convinced that the two types of slans should co-operate instead of fight."

"Don't be silly," she said. "Every slan we've ever caught was willing to promise anything."

The words were like so many blows, and Jommy Cross shrank from them, feeling beaten, his argument smashed. In his deepest thoughts, he had always pictured adult slans as noble creatures, dignified, contemptuous of captors, conscious of their marvellous superiority. But—willing to promise anything! He hurried on, desperately anxious to retrieve his position.

"That doesn't change this particular situation. You can verify practically everything I've said about myself. About my mother and father being killed. The fact that I had to flee the home of the old junk woman in the next room, whom you hit over the head, after I had lived with her ever since I was a child. Everything will fit in to prove that I am what I claim to be: a true slan who has never had any relationship with the secret slan organization. Can you lightly ignore the opportunity offered here? First, you and your people must help me find the slans, then I shall act as liaison officer, establish contact for you for the first time in your history. Tell me, have you ever learned why the true slans hate your people?"

"No." She spoke doubtfully. "We've had ridiculous statements from captured slans to the effect that they are simply not tolerating the existence of any variation of slan. Only the perfect result of Samuel Lann's machine must survive."

"Samuel . . . Lann's . . . machine!" Jommy Cross felt abruptly almost physically torn, his thread of thought ripped out by the roots. "Are you actually—do you mean it's true that slans were originally machine-made?"

He saw that the woman was staring at him, frowning, her brows sharply knit. She said slowly, "I'm almost beginning to believe your story. I thought every slan knew of Samuel Lann's use of a mutation machine on his wife. Later, during the nameless period that followed the slan war, use of the mutation machine produced a new species: the tendrilless slans. Didn't your parents find out anything about such things?"

"That was supposed to be my job," Jommy Cross said unhappily. "I was to do the exploring, the contacting, while Dad and Mother prepared the—"

He stopped in angry self-annoyance. This was no time to make an admission that his father had devoted his life to science and wouldn't waste a single day on a search he had believed would be long and difficult. The first mention of science might lead this acutely intelligent woman to an examination of his gun. She obviously believed the instrument to be a variation of her own electric-energy weapon. He went on:

"If those machines are still in existence, then all these human accusations that slans are making monsters out of human babies are true."

"I've seen some of the monsters," Joanna Hillory nodded. "Failures, of course. There are so many failures."

It seemed to Jommy Cross that he was past shock. All the things that he had believed for so long, believed with passion and pride, were tumbling like so many card houses. The ugly lies were not lies. Human beings were fighting a Machiavellian scourge almost inconceivable in its inhumanity. He grew aware that Joanna Hillory was talking.

"I must admit that, in spite of my conviction that the council will destroy you, the points you have raised do constitute a very particular situation. I have decided to take you before them."

It required a long moment for the meaning of her words to penetrate; and then—a wild, surging relief leaped along his nerves. It was like an intolerable weight lifting, lifting. There came an extravagant sense of buoyancy. At last he had what he needed so desperately: time, precious time! Given time, pure chance might aid him to escape.

He watched the woman as she moved cautiously over to the great instrument board. There was a click as her finger pressed a button. Her first words reached up, to the heights where his hopes poised, and dragged them to the uttermost low. She said:

84

"Calling the members of the council . . . Urgent . . . Please tune in at once to 7431 for immediate judgment on a special slan case."

Immediate judgment! He felt angry at himself for having had hope at all. He should have known that it wouldn't be necessary to take him physically before the council, when their radio science cancelled all dangers from such delay. Unless the council members understood a different logic than Joanna Hillory, he was through.

The waiting silence that followed was more apparent than real. There was the continuous thin, beating roar of the rockets, the fainter hiss of air against the outer shell which meant that the ship was still flying through the thick sheaf of Earth's atmosphere. And there was the insistent thought stream of Granny—the whole combining into anything but silence.

The impression smashed into fragments. Granny. Granny's active, *conscious* thought stream. Joanna Hillory, in meeting first his resistance, the pausing to question him instead of killing him instantly, had given Granny time to recuperate from the blow, which the slan woman had—obviously now—designed for temporary purposes only, to gain a silent approach on his rear. A killing blow might have made a distinct thud for ears as sensitive as his. The light one had not been effective for long. The old scoundrel was awake. Jommy opened his mind wide to the flood of Granny's thought.

"Jommy, she'll kill us both. But Granny's got a plan. Make some sign that you've heard her. Tap your feet. Jommy, Granny's got a plan to stop her from killing us."

Over and over came the insistent message, never quite the same, always accompanied by extraneous thought and uncontrollable digressions. No human brain as ill trained as Granny's could hold a completely straightforward thought. But the main theme was there. Granny was alive. Granny was aware of danger. And Granny was prepared to co-operate to desperate lengths to avert that danger.

Casually, Jommy Cross began to tap his feet on the floor, harder, louder, until—

"Granny hears." He stopped his tapping. Her excited thought went on: "Granny really has two plans. The first is for Granny to make a loud noise. That will startle the woman and give you a chance to leap on her. Then Granny will rush in to help. The second plan is for Granny to get up from the floor where she's lying, sneak over to your door, and then jump in at the woman when she passes near the door. She'll be startled, and instantly you can leap for her. Granny will call 'One', then 'Two!' Tap your feet after the plan number you think best. Think them over for a moment."

No thought was required. Plan One he instantly rejected. No loud noise would really distract the calm nerves of a slan. A physical attack, something concrete, was the only hope.

"One!" said Granny into his mind. He waited, ironically aware of the anxious overtones in her thought, the forlorn hope that he would find Plan One satisfactory and so lessen the danger to her own precious skin. But she was a practical old wretch, and deep in her brain was the conviction that Plan One was weak. At last her mind reluctantly pumped out the word "Two!"

Jommy Cross tapped his feet. Simultaneously, he grew aware that Joanna Hillory was talking into her radio, giving her history and his proposal of co-operation, finally offering her own opinion that he must be destroyed.

The remote thought came to Jommy Cross that a few minutes before he would have been sitting almost with bated breath following the discourse, and the answers that began to come in one by one from the hidden loudspeaker. Deep-toned voices of men; the rich, vibrant tones of women! But now he scarcely more than followed the thread of their arguments. He was aware of some disagreement. One of the women wanted to know his name. For a long moment it didn't strike him that he was being directly addressed:

"Your name?" said the radio voice.

Joanna Hillory moved away from the radio toward the door. She said sharply: "Are you deaf? She wants to know your name."

"Name!" said Jommy Cross, and a portion of his mind registered surprise at the question. But nothing could really distract him at this supreme moment. It was now or never. As he tapped his feet, every extraneous thought was gone out of his brain. He was only aware of Granny standing behind the door, and of the vibrations that poured from her. The tensing of her body, the poising for action and, at the last moment, terror. He waited helplessly while she stood there, her ravaged body threatened with paralysis.

It was the thousand illegal forays she had made in her black career that rose up to give her strength. She launched into the room. Eyes glittering, teeth bared, she lunged against the back of Joanna Hillory. Her thin arms embraced the arms and shoulders of the slan woman.

Flame sparkled as the weapon in Joanna Hillory's fingers discharged in futile fury at the floor. Then, like an animal, the young woman spun with irresistible strength. For one desperate moment Granny clung to her shoulders. It was the one all-necessary moment. In that instant, Jommy Cross sprang.

In that instant, too, came a shrill squawk from Granny. Her clawlike hands were torn from their holds, and the gaunt, dark body skidded along the floor.

Jommy Cross wasted no time trying to match a strength he felt sure was beyond his present powers to equal. As Joanna Hillory whirled toward him like a tigress, he struck one hard, swift blow across her neck with the edge of his hand. It was a dangerous blow; and it required perfect co-ordination of muscles and nerves. It could easily have broken her neck; instead, it skilfully and efficiently knocked her unconscious. He caught her as she fell, and even as he lowered her to the floor, his brain was reaching into hers, past the broken shield, searching swiftly. But the pulse of her unconscious brain was too slow, the kaleidoscope of pictures too frozen.

He began to shake her gently, watching the shifting pattern of her thoughts, as the steady physical movement brought quick subtle chemical changes in her body, which in turn changed the very shape of her thoughts. Still, there was no time for detail; and, as the outline of pictures grew more terrible in its menace, he abruptly deserted her and rushed to the radio. In as normal a voice as he could manage, he called:

"I'm still willing to discuss friendly terms. I could be a great help to the tendrilless slans." No answer. More urgently, he repeated his words, and added, "I'm anxious to come to an arrangement with an organization as powerful as yours. I'll even return the ship if you can show me logically how I can escape without putting myself into a trap."

Silence! He clicked off the radio, and turning, stared grimly at Granny, who was half sitting, half lying on the floor.

"No dice," he said. "All this, this ship, this slan woman, is only part of a trap in which nothing has been left to chance. There are seven heavily armed hundred-thousand-ton cruisers trailing us at this very moment. Their finder instruments react to our antigravity plates, so even the darkness is no protection. We're finished."

The hours of night dragged, and with each passing moment the problem of what to do grew more desperate. Of the four living things up there in that blue-black sky, only Granny sprawled in one of the pneumatic chairs in uneasy sleep. The two slans, and that tireless, throbbing, hurtling ship, remained awake.

Fantastic night! On the one hand was the knowledge of the destroying power that might strike at any minute; and on the other hand— Fascinated, Jommy Cross stared into the visiplate at the wondrous picture that sped beneath him. It was a world of lights, shining in every direction as far as the eye could see— lights and more lights. Splashes, pools, ponds, lakes, oceans of light—farm communities, villages, towns and cities, and, every little while, mile on mile of megalopolitan colossus. At last his gaze lifted from the visiplate and he turned to where Joanna

Hillory sat, her hands and feet tied. Her grey eyes met his brown ones questioningly. Before he could speak, she said:

"Well, have you decided yet?"

"Decided what?"

"When you're going to kill me, of course."

Jommy Cross shook his head slowly, gravely. "To me," he said quietly, "the appalling thing about your words is the mental attitude that assumes that one must either deliver or receive death. I'm not going to kill you. I'm going to release you."

She was silent for a moment, then: "There's nothing surprising about my attitude. For a hundred years the true slans killed my people at sight; for hundreds of years now we have retaliated. What could be more natural?"

Jommy Cross shrugged impatiently. There was too much uncertainty in him about the true slans to permit him to discuss them now when his whole mind must be concentrated on escape. He said:

"My interest is not in this futile, miserable, three-cornered war among human beings and slans. The important thing is the seven warships that are trailing us at this minute."

"It's too bad you found out about them," the slan woman said quietly. "Now you will spend the time in useless worry and planning. It would have been so much less cruel for you to have considered yourself safe and, then, the very moment you discovered you were not, to die."

"I'm not dead yet!" Jommy Cross said, and impatience was suddenly sharp in his tone. "I have no doubt it is presumptuous of a half-grown slan to assume, as I am beginning to, that there must be a way out of this trap. I have the greatest respect for adult slan intelligence, but I do not forget that your people have now suffered several preliminary defeats. Why, for instance, if my destruction is so certain, are those ships waiting? Why wait?"

Joanna Hillory was smiling, her fine, strong face relaxed. "You don't really expect me to answer your questions, do you?"

"Yes." Jommy Cross smiled, but without humour. He went on in a tight, clipped voice, "You see, I've grown somewhat older during the past few hours. Until last night I was really very innocent, very idealistic. For instance, during those first few minutes when we were pointing our guns at each other, you could have destroyed me without resistance on my part. To me, you were a member of the slan race, and all slans must be united. I couldn't have pulled the trigger to save my soul. You delayed, of course, because you wanted to question me, but the opportunity was there. That situation exists no longer."

The woman's perfect lips pursed in sudden, frowning thought. "I think I'm beginning to see what you're getting at."

"It's really very simple," Jommy Cross nodded grimly. "You

either answer my questions or I'll knock you over the head and obtain the information from your unconscious mind."

The woman began: "How do you know I'll tell the tru—" She stopped, her grey eyes widening with apprehension as she glared at Jommy. "Do *you* expect—"

"I do!" He stared ironically into her glowing, hostile eyes. "You will lower your mind shield. Of course, I don't expect absolutely free access to your brain. I have no objection to your controlling your thoughts on a narrow range all around the subject. But your shield must go down—now!"

She sat very still, body rigid, grey eyes agleam with repugnance. Jommy Cross' gaze was curious.

"I'm amazed," he said. "What strange complexes develop in minds that have no direct contact with other minds. Is it possible that tendrilless slans have built up little sacred, secret worlds within themselves and, like any sensitive human being, feel shame at letting outsiders see that world? There is material here for psychological study that may reveal the basic cause of the slan-versus-slan war. However, let that go."

He finished, "Remember that I have already been in your mind. Remember, also, that according to your own logic, in a few hours I will be blotted out forever in a blaze of electric projectors."

"Of course," she said quickly, "that is true. You will be dead, won't you? Very well, I'll answer your questions."

Joanna Hillory's mind was like a book whose thickness could not be measured, with almost an infinity of pages to examine, an incredibly rich, incredibly complex structure embroidered with a billion billion impressions garnered through the years by an acutely observant intellect. Jommy Cross caught swift, tantalizing glimpses of her recent experiences. There was, briefly, the picture of an unutterably bleak planet, low-mountained, sandy, frozen, everything frozen—Mars! There were pictures of a gorgeous, glass-enclosed city, of great machines digging under a blazing battery of lights. Somewhere it was snowing with a bitter, unearthly fury—and a black spaceship, glittering like a dark jewel in the sun, was briefly visible through a thick plate-glass window.

The confusion of thoughts cleared as she began to talk. She spoke slowly, and he made no attempt to hurry her, in spite of his conviction that every second counted, that at any minute now death would blast from the sky at his defenceless ship. Her words and the thoughts that verified them were as bright-cut as so many gems, and as fascinating.

The tendrilless slans had known from the moment he started to climb the wall that an interloper was coming. Interested primarily in his purpose, they made no effort to stop him when he could have been destroyed without difficulty. They left several ways open for him to get to the ship, and he had used one of them, although—and here was an unknown, unexpected factor—the particular alarms of that way had not gone off.

The reason the warships were slow in destroying him was that they hesitated to use their searchlights over a continent so densely inhabited. If he should climb high enough or go out to sea, the ship would be quickly destroyed. On the other hand, if he chose to circle around on the continent, his fuel would waste away in a dozen hours or so, and before that, dawn would come and enable the electric projectors to be used with brief, deadly effect.

"Suppose," said Jommy Cross, "I should land in the downtown section of a great city. I could very possibly escape among so many houses, buildings, and people."

Joanna Hillory shook her head. "If this ship's speed falls below two hundred miles per hour, it will be destroyed, regardless of the risk involved, regardless of the fact that they hope to save my life by capturing the ship intact. You can see I'm being very frank with you."

Jommy Cross was silent. He was convinced, overwhelmed by the totality of the danger. There was nothing clever about the plan. Here was simply a crude reliance on big guns and plenty of them. "All this," he marvelled at last, "for one poor slan, one ship. How mighty the fear must be that prompts so much effort, so much expense, for so little return!"

"We have put the snake outside our law," came the cool reply. Her grey eyes glowed with a quiet fire. Her mind concentrated on the single track of her words. "Human courts do not release prisoners because it will cost more to convict them than the amount of the theft. Besides, what you have stolen is so precious that it would be the greatest disaster in our history if you escaped."

He felt abruptly impatient. "You assume far too readily that the true slans are not already in possession of the antigravity secret. My purpose during the coming years is to analyse the true slans to their hiding place; and I can tell you now that practically everything you have told me I shall not use as evidence. The very fact that they are so completely hidden is an indication of their immense resourcefulness."

Joanna Hillory said, "Our logic is very simple. We have not seen them in rocketships—so they have no rocketships. Even yesterday, in that ridiculous flight to the palace, their craft, while very pretty, was powered by multiple-pulse jet motors, a type of engine we discarded a hundred years ago. Logic, like science, is deduction on the basis of observation, so—"

Jommy Cross frowned unhappily. Everything about the slans

was wrong. They were fools and murderers. They had started a stupid, ruthless, fratricidal war against the tendrilless slans. They sneaked around the country, using their diabolical mutation machines on human mothers—and the monstrosities that resulted were destroyed by medical authorities. Mad, purposeless destruction! And it simply didn't fit!

It didn't fit with the noble character of his father and his mother. It didn't fit with his father's genius, or with the fact that for six years he himself had lived under the influence of Granny's squalid mind and remained untouched, unsoiled. And, finally, it didn't fit with the fact that he, a half-grown true slan, had braved a trap he did not even suspect and because of one loophole in their net, one unknown factor, had so far escaped their vengeance.

His atomic gun! The one factor that they still didn't suspect. It would be useless, of course, against the battle cruisers coasting along in the blackness behind him. It would take a year or more to build a projector with a beam big enough to reach out and tear those ships to pieces. But one thing it could do. What it *could* touch, its shattering fire would disintegrate into component atoms. And, by God! he had the answer, given time and a little luck.

The glare of a searchlight splashed against his visiplates. Simultaneously, the ship jumped like some toy that had been struck an intolerable blow. Metal squeaked, walls shook, lights blinked, and then, as the sounds of violence died into little menacing whispers, he bounded from the deeps of the chair into which he had been flung and snatched at the rocket activator.

The machine leaped forward in dizzy acceleration. Against the pressure of plunging fury, he reached forward and clicked on the radio.

The battle was on, and unless he could persuade them to desist, the chance to put his one lone plan into action would never come. The rich, vibrant voice of Joanna Hillory echoed the thought that beat in his mind.

"What are you going to do—talk them out of what they plan to do? Don't be so silly. If they finally decided to sacrifice me, you don't think they'd give *your* welfare any consideration, do you?"

11

Outside, the night sky was dark. A sprinkling of stars glittered coldly in the moonless night. There was no sign of an enemy ship, not a shadow, not a movement against the immensity of turgid, deep, deep blue ceiling.

Inside, the tense silence was shattered by a hoarse choking cry from the next room. An angry barrage of vituperation followed. Granny was awake.

"What's the matter? What's happened?"

Brief silence, and then abrupt end of anger and mad beginning of fear. Instantly, her terrified thought poured out in frantic flood. Obscene curses, born of fear, assailed the air. Granny didn't want to die. Kill all slans, but not Granny. Granny had money to—

She was drunk. The sleep had allowed the liquor to take control of her again. Jommy Cross shut her thoughts and her voice out of his mind. Urgently he spoke into the radio.

"Calling the commander of the warships! Calling the commander! Joanna Hillory is alive. I am willing to release her at dawn, the only condition being that I be allowed to get up into the air again."

There was silence, then a woman's quiet voice entered the room. "Joanna, are you there?"

"Yes, Marian."

"Very well," the calm voice of the other went on, "we accept on the following conditions: You will inform us an hour before the actual landing where it will be. The point of landing must be at least thirty miles—that is, five minutes allowing for acceleration and deceleration—from the nearest large city. We assume, of course, that you believe you can escape. Very well. You will have two hours more of opportunity. We shall have Joanna Hillory. A fair exchange!"

"I accept," said Jommy Cross.

"Wait!" cried Joanna Hillory. But Jommy Cross was too quick for her. A second before the word jerked from her lips, his finger flicked off the radio switch.

He whirled on her. "You shouldn't have put up your mind shield. It was all the warning I needed. But, of course, I had you either way. If you hadn't put up the shield, I would have caught the thought in your brain." His eyes glinted at her suspiciously.

"What is this sudden mad passion to sacrifice yourself simply to deny me two hours more of life?"

She was silent. Her grey eyes were more thoughtful than he had seen them all night. He mocked gently:

"Can it be that you actually grant me the possibility of escape?"

"I've been wondering," she said, "why the alarms back in the spaceship building didn't warn us of the exact way you approached this ship. There is a factor here that apparently we did not take into account. If you should really escape with this ship—"

"I shall escape," Jommy Cross said quietly, "and I shall live in spite of human beings, in spite of Kier Gray and John Petty and the ghoulish crew of murderers that live in the palace. I shall live in spite of the vastness of the tendrilless slan organization and their murderous intentions. And someday I shall find the true slans. Not now, for no youth can hope to succeed where the tendrilless slans in their thousands have failed. But I shall find them, and on that day—" He stopped, then gravely: "Miss Hillory, I want to assure you that neither this nor any other ship will ever be turned against your people."

"You speak very rashly," she replied with sudden bitterness. "How can you assure anything in the name of those ruthless creatures who dominate the councils of the snakes?"

Jommy Cross gazed down at the woman. There was truth in her words. And yet, something of the greatness that was to be his came to him in that moment as he sat there in that finely built control room, with its glittering instrument board, the shining visiplates, his body deep in the beautifully constructed chair. He was his father's son, heir to the products of his father's genius. Given time, he would be lord of irresistible power. The soft flame of those thoughts was in his voice as he said:

"Madam, in all modesty I can say that, of all the slans in the world today, there is none more important than the son of Peter Cross. Wherever I go my words and my will shall have influence. The day that I find the true slans, the war against your people will end forever. You have said that my escape would be disaster for the tendrilless slans; rather, it will be their greatest victory. Someday you and they will realize that."

"Meanwhile," the slan woman smiled grimly, "you have two hours to escape seven heavy cruisers owned by the real rulers of the Earth. What you do not seem to realize is that we actually fear neither human being nor snake, that our organization is vast beyond imagination. Every village, every town, every city has its quota of tendrilless slans. We know our power, and one of these days we shall come out into the open, take control and—"

"It would mean war!" Jommy Cross flared.

Her answer was cold. "We'll smash everything they've got within two months."

"And then what? What about human beings in that afterworld? Do you contemplate four billion slaves in perpetuity?"

"We are immeasurably their superiors. Shall *we* live in endless hiding, endure privation on the colder planets when we long for the green Earth and freedom from this eternal fight against nature—and against the men whom you defend so valiantly? We owe *them* nothing but pain. Circumstances force us to repay with interest!"

Jommy Cross said, "I foresee disaster for everyone."

The woman shrugged and went on: "The factor that worked in your favour back at the Air Centre, when our attitude was the negative one of waiting for events, cannot possibly help you now, when our attitude is the utterly positive one of destroying you with our heaviest weapons. One minute of fire will burn this machine to ashes that will fall to earth in a fine sprinkling of dust."

"One minute!" Jommy Cross exclaimed.

He stopped short. He hadn't dreamed the time limit would be so short, and that now he had to depend on a flimsy psychological hope that the speed of his ship would lull their suspicions. He said harshly:

"Enough of this damn talk. And I'll have to carry you into the next room. I've got to rig up a vice at the inside of the nose of the ship, and I can't let you see what I put in that vice."

For a moment before Jommy Cross landed he saw the lights of the city to the west. Then the wall of a valley blotted the flashing sea of brilliance from his view. Soft as thistledown, the rocketship touched the ground and floated there with an unearthly buoyancy as Jommy Cross set the antigravity plates at balancing power. He clicked open the door and then untied the slan woman.

Her electric gun in hand (his own weapon was fastened in the vise he had set up), he watched Joanna Hillory poised for a moment in the doorway. Dawn was breaking over the hills to the east, and the light, still a sickly grey, made a queer silhouette of her strong, shapely figure. Without a word, she jumped to the ground below. As he stepped forward to the threshold he could see her head on a level now with the bottom of the doorway, reflecting the flood of light from inside the ship.

Her head turned, and the face that looked up at him was marked by deep, thoughtful lines. She said, "How do you feel?"

He shrugged. "A little shaky, but death seems remote and not applicable to me."

"It's more than that," was the earnest reply. "The nervous system of a slan is an almost impregnable fortress. It cannot really be touched by insanity or 'nerves' or fear. When we kill,

94

it is because of policy arrived at through logic. When death approaches our personal lives, we accept the situation, fight to the last in the hope of an unpredictable factor turning up to save us, and finally, reluctantly, give up the ghost, conscious that we have not lived in vain."

He stared at her curiously, his mind projecting against hers, feeling of the gentle pulsing of overtones, the strange half friendliness that was in her voice and overflowed from her mind. His eyes narrowed. What purpose was forming in her alert, sensitive, unsentimental brain? She went on:

"Jommy Cross, it may surprise you to know that I have come to believe your story, and that you are not only what you say you are, but that you actually hold the ideals you have professed. You are the first true slan I have ever met and, for the first time in my life, I have a sense of tension eased, as if, after all these centuries, the deadly darkness is lifting. If you escape our guns, I beg you to keep your ideals as you grow older, and please don't betray us. Don't become a tool of creatures who have used only murder and destruction for so many, many years. You have been in my mind, and you know that I have not lied to you about them. Whatever the logic of their philosophy, it's wrong because it's inhuman. It must be wrong because its result has been unending misery."

If he escaped! So that was it! If he escaped, they would be dependent on his good will, and she was playing that angle now for all she was worth.

"But remember one thing," Joanna Hillory went on; "you can expect no help from us. We must, in the name of security, consider you as an enemy. Too much depends upon it, the fate of too many people is involved. So do not expect at some future date to obtain mercy, Jommy Cross, because of what I have said or because you have released me. Do not come into our midst, because, I warn you, it means swift death.

"You see, we credit true slans with superior intelligence, or rather, superior development of intelligence, owing to their mind-reading ability. There is no cunning of which we would not believe them capable, no ruthlessness they have not already equalled. A plan requiring thirty or a hundred years to mature is not beyond them. Therefore, even though I believe what you have told me, the uncertainty of how you may develop as you grow older would make me kill you this instant were it in my power. Do not ever test our good will. It is suspicion, not tolerance, that rules us. But now, good-by and, paradoxical as this may sound, good luck!"

He watched her as she walked lightly, swiftly, into the darkness that lay heavily on the valley to the west, the way that led to the city—his way, also. Her form became a shadow in the clinging mist of night. She was gone over a hill. Swiftly, he closed the door, rushed into the storeroom and snatched a couple of space suits from the wall. The old woman babbled in feeble protest as he stuffed her forcibly into one of them. He crowded into his own as he scrambled into the control room.

He closed the door on the sobering leer that twisted Granny's face behind the transparent headpiece, and in a second was sitting tensely staring into the "sky" visiplate. His fingers reached for the activator of the antigravity plates; and then came the hesitation, the doubt that had been growing in him each second that brought the inexorable moment of action nearer. Was it possible that his simple plan would actually work?

Jommy Cross could see the ships, little dark spots in the sky above him. The sun was shining up there, a spray of brilliance that picked out the tiny torpedo shapes like so many fly spots on an immense blue ceiling. The clouds and the haze of the valley were clearing with magical speed, and if the clarity with which he could see them through his visiplates was any criterion, then even the weather was against him. He was still in the shadows of this sweet, clean little valley, but in a few minutes now the very perfection of the day would begin to damage his chances of escape.

His brain was so tensely concentrated that for a moment the distorted thought that flowed into his mind seemed to come from himself:

". . . needn't worry. Old Granny'll get rid of the slan. Get some make-up and change her face. What's the good of having been an actress if you can't change your looks? Granny'll make a white, lovely body like she used to have, and change this old face. Ugh!"

She seemed to spit in convulsions at the thought of her face, and Jommy Cross eased the picture out of his mind. But her words remained with him. His parents had used false hair, but the necessary mutilation of natural hair and the constant recutting had proved very unsatisfactory. Nevertheless, true slans must be doing it all the time, and now that he was old enough to be able to make a reasonably efficient job of it, with Granny's help and experience it might be the answer.

Strangely, now that a plan for the future had come, his hesitation vanished. Light as a dust mote, the ship fell away from Earth, and then jerked into enormous speed as the rockets kicked into life. Five minutes to accelerate and decelerate, the slan commander had said. Jommy Cross smiled grimly. He wasn't going to decelerate. At undiminished speed, he dived for the river that made a wide black swath at the outskirts of the city, the city he had picked because the river was there. At the very last moment he put on full deceleration.

And at that final moment, when it was already too late, the confidence of the slan commanders must have been shaken. They forgot their reluctance to use their guns and show their ships so near a human city. They swooped like great birds of prey; fire sparkled from all seven cruisers. . . . Jommy Cross pulled gently on the wire that pressed the trigger on his own weapon, mounted in the vise at the nose of the ship.

From outside, a violent blow added speed to the three-hundred-miles-an-hour clip of his machine. But he scarcely noticed it, the only effect of the enemy fire. His attention was concentrated on his own weapon. As he pulled the wire there was a flare of white. Instantly a two-foot circle in the thick nose of the craft vanished. The white, malignant ray leaped forth fanwise, dissolving the water of the river in front of the torpedo-shaped craft, and into the tunnel thus created slid the spaceship, decelerating at full, frightful blast of the forward tubes.

The visiplates went black with the water above and the water below, then blacker as the water ended and the inconceivable ferocity of the atom smasher bored on irresistibly into the ground beyond, deeper, deeper.

It was like flying through air, only there was no resistance except the pressure of rocket blasts. The atoms of earth, broken into their component elements, instantly lost their mathematically unreal solidity and assumed their actuality of a space tenuously occupied by matter. Ten million million years of built-up cohesion collapsed into the lowest state of primeval matter.

With rigid gaze, Jommy Cross stared at the second hand of his watch: ten, twenty, thirty . . . one minute. He began to ease the nose of the ship upward, but the enormous pressure of deceleration made no physical easing possible. It was thirty seconds before he cut the number of rocket blasts and the end was in sight.

After two minutes and twenty seconds of underground flight the ship stopped. He must be near the centre of the city, and there was approximately eight miles of tunnel behind him, into which water would be pouring from the tortured river. The water would close up the hole, but the frustrated tendrilless slans would need no interpreter to tell them what had happened. Besides, their instruments would this very second be pointing directly at the location of his ship.

Jommy Cross laughed joyously. Let them know. What could they hope to do to him now? There was danger ahead, of course —immense danger, especially when he and Granny reached the surface. The entire tendrilless slan organization must be warned by this time. Nevertheless, that was of the future. For the moment, victory was his, and it was sweet, after so many desperate, tiring hours. Now there was Granny's plan, which involved his separating from her, and disguise.

The laughter faded from his lips. He sat thoughtful, then stalked into the adjoining compartment. The black moneybag he wanted lay on the old woman's lap under the protection of one clawlike hand. Before she could even realize his intention, he had snatched it up. Granny shrieked and jumped at him. Coolly he held her off.

"Don't get excited. I've decided to adopt your plan. I'll try to get by disguised as a human being, and we'll separate. I'm going to give you five thousand of this. The rest you'll get back about a year from now. Here's what you're to do:

"I need a place to live, and so you're going to go up into the mountains and buy a ranch or something. When you're located, put an ad in the local paper. I'll put an answering ad in, and we'll get together. I'll keep the money just in case you decide to double-cross me. Sorry, but you captured me in the first place, and so you'll just have to bear with me. But now I've got to go back and block that tunnel. Someday I'm going to fit this ship with atomic energy, and I don't want them coming here meanwhile."

He'd have to leave this city swiftly, of course, for the time being, the beginning of a continental tour. There must be other tendrilled slans out there. Just as his mother and father had met accidentally, pure chance alone should enable him to meet at least one slan. And besides, there was the first investigation to be made on the still vague though great plan that was taking form in his brain. The plan to *think* his way to the true slans.

12

HE SEARCHED—and he worked. In the quiet fastness of his laboratory on Granny's valley ranch, the plans and projects that his father had impressed upon him were slowly brought to reality. In a hundred ways he learned to control the limitless energy that he held in trust for slans and human beings alike.

He discovered that the effectiveness of his father's invention resulted from two basic facts: the source of power could be as tiny as a few grains of matter; and the output need not take the form of heat.

It could be converted to motion and to vibration, to radiation and—directly—to electricity.

He began to build himself an arsenal. He transformed a mountain near the ranch into a fortress, knowing that it would be inadequate against any concerted attack, but it was something. With an ever vaster protective science behind him, his search grew more determined.

Jommy Cross seemed always to be driving along roads that gleamed toward distant horizons, or in strange cities, each with its endless swarms of human beings. The sun rose and set, and rose and set, and there were dark days of drizzling rains, and there were countless nights. Although he was always alone, loneliness did not touch him, for his expanding soul fed with an always dissatisfied eagerness at the tremendous drama that was daily enacted before his eyes. Everywhere he turned, facets of the tendrilless slan organization met his gaze, and week by week he grew more puzzled. Where were the true slans?

The puzzle seemed a crazy, unanswerable thing that never left him. It followed him now as he walked slowly up a street of the hundredth—or was it the thousandth?—city.

Night lay upon the city, night spattered by countless glittering shop windows and a hundred million blazing lights. He walked to a newsstand and bought all the local papers, then back to his car, that very ordinary-looking, very special battleship on wheels which he never allowed out of his sight. He stood beside the long, low-built machine. A chilling night wind caught at the sheets of the paper as he turned page after page, briefly letting his gaze skim down the columns.

The wind grew colder as he stood there, bringing the damp-sweet smell of rain. A gust of cold air caught an edge of his paper, whipped it madly for a moment, abruptly tore it, then went screaming victoriously down the street, chasing the scrap of paper wildly. He folded the newspaper decisively against the rising clamour of wind and climbed into the car. An hour later he tossed the seven daily papers into a sidewalk wastepaper receptacle. Deep in thought, he re-entered the car and sat behind the steering wheel.

The same old story. Two of the papers were tendrilless slan. It was easy for his mind to note the subtle difference, the special coloration of the articles, the very way the words were used, the distinct difference between the human-owned papers and those operated by the tendrilless slans. Two papers out of seven. But those two had the highest circulation. It was a normal average.

And, once more, that was all there was. Human being and tendrilless slan. No third group, none of the difference that he knew would show him when a paper was operated by true slans, if his theory were right. It remained only to obtain all the weekly papers, and to spend the evening as he had spent the day, driving along the streets, searching each house, each passing mind; and then, as he drove toward the distant east, the gathering tempest charged like some untamed beast through the black night.

Behind him, the night and the storm swallowed up another city, another failure.

The water lay dark and still around the spaceship in that third year when Jommy Cross finally returned to the tunnel. He swirled around in the mud, turning the blazing force of his atomic-powered machines on the wounded metal thing.

Ten-point steel seared over the hole his disintegrator had carved on that day when he escaped the slan cruisers. And all through one almost endless week a snug-fitting, leech-shaped metal monstrosity hugged inch by inch over the surface of the ship, straining with its frightful power at the very structure of the atoms, till the foot-thick walls of the long, sleek machine were ten-point steel from end to end.

It took him some weeks to analyse the antigravity plates with their electrically built-up vibrations, and to fashion a counter-part which, with grim irony, he left there in the tunnel, for it was on them that the detectors of the tendrilless slans operated. Let them think their craft still there.

Three months he slaved and then, in the dead of one cold October night, the ship backed along six miles of tunnel on a cushion of resistless atomic drive, and plunged up through a mist of icy rain.

The rain became sleet, then snow; then abruptly he was beyond the clouds, beyond earth's petty furies. Above him the vast canopy of the heavens glittered in a blazing array of stars that beckoned to his matchless ship. There was Sirius, the brightest jewel in that diadem, and there was Mars, the red. But it was not for Mars that he was heading today. This was only a short exploratory voyage, a cautious trip to the Moon, a test flight to provide that all-necessary experience which his logic would use as a basis for the long, dangerous journey that seemed to be becoming more inevitable with each passing month of his utterly futile search. Someday he would have to go to Mars.

Beneath him a blur of night-enveloped globe receded. At one edge of that mass, a blaze of light grew more brilliant as he watched and then, abruptly, his contemplation of the glory of the approaching sunrise was jarred by the clanging of an alarm bell. A pointer light flashed on and off discordantly far up on his forward visiplate. Decelerating at full speed, he watched the changing position of the light. Suddenly, the light clicked off and there, at the extreme range of his vision, was a ship.

The battleship was not coming directly toward him. It grew larger, became plainly visible just beyond the Earth's shadow, in the full glare of the Sun. It passed by him, less than a hundred miles away, a thousand-foot structure of smooth, dark metal. It plunged into the shadows and instantly vanished. In half an hour the alarm stopped ringing.

And then, ten minutes later, it was clamouring again. The second ship was farther away, travelling at right angles to the path of the first. It was a smaller ship by far, destroyer size, and it did not follow a fixed path, but darted here and there.

When it was gone in the distance, Jommy Cross edged his ship forward, undecided now, almost awed. A battleship and a destroyer! Why? It seemed to indicate a patrol. But against whom? Not against human beings, surely. They didn't even know the tendrilless slans and their ships existed.

He slowed his ship, stopped. He was not prepared yet to risk running a gauntlet of well-equipped battleships. Watchfully, he swung his ship around—and in the middle of the turn he saw the small dark object, like a meteorite, rushing toward him.

In a flash he whipped aside. The object twisted after him like a living monster out of space. It loomed far up in his rear visiplate, a dark, round metal ball, about a yard in diameter. Frantically, Jommy Cross tried to manoeuvre his ship out of its path, but before he could make a turn there was a deafening, mind-shattering blast.

The explosion smashed him to the floor; the concussion kept him there, stunned, sick but still alive, and conscious that those sturdy walls had survived the almost intolerable blow. The ship was rocking in frightful acceleration. Dizzily, Jommy Cross picked himself up and climbed back into the control chair.

He'd struck a mine. A floating mine! What terrifying precautions were here—and against what?

Thoughtfully he manoeuvred his dented, almost disabled ship into a tunnel under the river that cut through Granny's ranch, a tunnel that curved up into the heart of a mountain peak, clear of the water that swirled after it. He could not even hazard a guess as to how long it must remain hidden there. Its outer walls were violently radioactive and therefore the ship was temporarily useless to him if only for that reason. And one other thing was certain. He was not ready yet either to oppose or to outwit the tendrilless slans.

Two days later, Jommy Cross stood in the doorway of the rambling ranch house and watched their nearest neighbour, Mrs. Lanahan, come tight-lipped along the pathway that led between the two orchards. She was a plump blonde whose round baby face concealed a prying, malicious mind. Her blue eyes glowed at Granny's tall, brown-eyed, brown-haired grandson with suspicion.

Jommy Cross eyed her with amusement as he opened the door for her and followed her into the house. In her mind was all the ignorance of those who had lived their lives in backward rural areas in a world where education had become a pale shadow, a weak, characterless reflection of official cynicism. She didn't know exactly what a slan was, but she thought he was one, and she was there to find out. She made an interesting experiment for his crystal method of hypnotism. It was fascinating to watch the way she kept glancing at the tiny crystal he had put on the table beside her chair—observing the way she talked on, completely in character, never realizing when she ceased to be a free agent and became his slave.

She walked out finally into the glare of the late fall sunshine, apparently unchanged. But the errand that had brought her to the farmhouse was forgotten, for her mind was conditioned to a new attitude toward slans. Not hatred—that was for a possible future that Jommy Cross could envision; and not approval—that was for her own protection in a world of slan haters.

The following day he saw her husband, a black-bearded giant of a man in a distant field. A quiet talk, a differently attuned crystal, brought him, also, under control.

During the months that he relaxed with the hypnotically sweetened old woman that had been Granny, he gained mental control of every one of the hundreds of farm people who dwelt in the idyllic climate of the valley there in the ever-green foothills. At first he needed the crystals, but as his knowledge of the human mind grew, he found that, although it was a slower process, he could entirely dispense with that atomically unbalanced glass.

He estimated: Even at the rate of two thousand hypnotized

a year, and not allowing for new generations, he could hypnotize the four billion people in the world in two million years. Conversely, two million slans could do it in a year, provided they possessed the secret of his crystals.

Two million needed, and he couldn't even find one. Somewhere there *must* be a true slan. And during the years that still must pass before he could logically pit his intelligence against the intellectual task involved in finding the true slan organization, he must search and search for that one.

13

SHE WAS TRAPPED. Briefly, Kathleen Layton grew tense. Her slim young body straightened there beside the open drawer of Kier Gray's desk, the contents of which she had been studying. Her mind reached out with startled alertness, through intervening doors, to where Kier Gray and another man were opening the door that led from her room through a corridor and another room to this, the dictator's own study.

She was conscious of chagrin. For weeks she had waited for the council meeting that would claim Kier Gray's attendance and give her safe access to his study—and now this wild accident. For the first time in her experience, Kier Gray had gone to her room instead of summoning her to him. With all the other exits guarded, her one avenue of escape had been cut off.

She was trapped! Yet she did not regret her action in coming. An imprisoned slan could have no purpose but escape. The seriousness of her position struck deeper instant by instant. To be caught here red-handed— Abruptly, she ceased putting the papers back into the drawer. No time. The men were just beyond the door now.

With sudden decision she closed the drawer, jerked the papers into a rough pile at one side of the desk and, like a fleeing fawn, rushed to an easy chair. Simultaneously, the door opened, and John Petty came in, followed by Kier Gray. The two men stopped as they saw her. The police chief's handsome face took on a darker colour. His eyes narrowed to slits, then his gaze flicked questioningly to the dictator. The leader's eyebrows were lifted quizzically, and there was the faintest hint of irony in the smile that came into his face.

"Hullo," he said. "What brings you here?"

Kathleen had come to a decision about that, but before she could speak, John Petty cut in. The man had a beautiful voice when he wanted to use it, and he used it now. He said gently:

"She's obviously been spying on you, Kier."

There was something about this man with his incisive logic that brought chilling alarm to the girl. It seemed to be the dark destiny of the secret-police chief to be present at the critical moments of her life, and she knew with a stiffening of her courage that here was such a moment, and that of all the people in the world, John Petty would strive with the full passion of his hatred for her to make it deadly.

The police head went on calmly, "Really, Kier, we come dramatically back to what we were discussing. Next week this slan girl will be twenty-one years of age, for all legal purposes an adult. Is she to live on here until she eventually dies of old age a hundred and fifty or some such fantastic term of years from now? Or what?"

The smile on Kier Gray's face was grimmer. "Kathleen, didn't you know I was at the council meeting?"

"You bet she knew," John Petty interjected, "and its unexpected ending came as an unpleasant surprise."

Kathleen said coldly, "I refuse to make replies to any questioning in which that man participates. He's trying to keep his voice calm and logical but, in spite of the queer way in which he hides his thoughts, there is already a distinct glow of excitement streaming from him. And the thought has come to the surface of his mind that at last he will be able to convince you that I ought to be destroyed."

The leader's face was oddly hostile in the thoughtfulness that came into it. Her mind touched lightly at the surface of his brain, and there was a forming thought there, a developing decision, impossible to read. He said finally:

"Historically speaking, her charge against you is true, John. Your desire for her death is . . . er . . . proved—a tribute, of course, to your antislan zeal, but a queer fanaticism in so enormously capable a man."

John Petty seemed to shake off the words in the impatient gesture he made. "The truth is, I want her dead, and I don't want her dead. To me she constitutes a grave menace to the State, located here in the palace and possessing mind-reading ability. I simply want her out of the way; and, being unsentimental about slans, I consider death the most effective method. However, I will not urge such a verdict in view of my reputation for bias in this case. But I seriously think that my suggestion at the meeting today is a good one. She should be moved to a different residence."

There was no thought near the surface of Kier Gray's mind to suggest that he intended to speak. His gaze was on her with unnecessary steadiness. Kathleen said scathingly:

"The moment I am removed from this palace, I will be murdered. As Mr. Gray said in effect ten years ago, after *your* hireling tried to murder me, once a slan is dead, inquiries into the affair are viewed with suspicion."

She saw that Kier Gray was shaking his head at her. He spoke in the mildest, most unconvincing tone she had ever heard him use. "You assume far too readily, Kathleen, that I cannot protect you. On the whole, I think it is the best plan."

She stared at him, stiff with dismay. He finished the virtual death sentence, his voice no longer mild, but even-toned, decisive:

"You will gather your clothes and possessions and prepare yourself for departure in twenty-four hours."

The shock passed. Her mind grew quite calm. The knowledge that Kier Gray had withdrawn his protection from her was too crystal-clear a realization for her to require any anticlimax of emotional disbelief.

What astounded her was that there was as yet no evidence on which he could have based a criminal judgment. He hadn't even glanced at the papers she had arranged so hurriedly on the desk. Therefore, his decision was based on the mere fact of her presence here and on John Petty's accusations.

Which was surprising, because he had in the past defended her from Petty under far more sinister circumstances. And she had come unpunished, unchecked into this study on at least half a dozen other occasions.

It meant that his decision had been previously made, and therefore was beyond any argument she could hope to offer. She grew aware that there was amazement, too, in John Petty's brain. The man was frowning at his easy victory. The surface of his mind vibrated briefly a small stream of dissatisfaction, then abrupt decision to clinch the matter. His gaze flicked keenly over the room and came to rest on the desk.

"The point is, what did she find out while she was alone in your study? What are those papers?" He was not a shy man; and even while he asked the question he was stalking to the desk. As the leader came over behind him, Petty rippled through the sheets. "Hm-m-m, the list of all the old slan hide-outs which we still use for trapping the unorganized slans. Fortunately, there are so many hundreds of them that she couldn't have had time to memorize their names, let alone descriptions of their locations."

The falseness of his conclusion was not what concerned Kathleen in that moment of discovery. Evidently neither man suspected that not only was the location of every one of the slan hideaways imprinted indelibly on her mind, but that she had an almost photographic record of the alarm systems which the secret police had installed in each unit to warn them when an unsuspecting slan was entering. According to the shrewd analysis of one report, there must be some kind of thought broadcaster which made it possible for strange slans to locate the hiding places. But that was unimportant just now.

What counted was Kier Gray. The leader was staring curiously at the papers. "This is more serious than I thought," he said slowly, and Kathleen's heart sank. "She's been searching through my desk."

Kathleen thought tensely: It wasn't necessary for him to let

John Petty know that. The old Kier Gray would never have provided her worst enemy with an ounce of ammunition to use against her.

Kier Gray's eyes were cold as he turned to her. Strangely, the surface of his brain showed as calm and cool as she had ever known it to be. He was, she realized, not angry but, with an icy finality, breaking with her.

"You will go to your room and pack—and await further instructions."

She was turning away as John Petty said, "You have said on various occasions, sir, that you were keeping her alive for observation purposes only. If you move her from your presence, that purpose is no longer applicable. Therefore, I hope I am safe in assuming that she will be placed under the protection of the secret police."

Kathleen shut her mind to their two minds as she closed the door behind her and raced along the corridor to her room. She felt not the vaguest interest in the details of any hypocritical murder plan which might be worked out between the leader and his henchman. Her course was clear. She opened the door leading from her room to one of the main corridors, nodded to the guard, who acknowledged her greeting stiffly—and then she walked calmly to the nearest elevator.

Theoretically, she was only allowed to go to the five-hundred-foot level, and not to the plane hangars, five hundred feet farther up. But the stocky young soldier who operated the elevator proved no match for the blow that struck him slantingly on the jaw. Like most of the other men, Kathleen saw in his mind, he had never accepted the idea that this tall, slender girl was dangerous to a two-hundred-pound male in the prime of strength. He was unconscious before he discovered his mistake. It was cruel, but she tied his hands and feet with wire and used wire to tie the gag she placed in his mouth.

Arrived at the roof, she made a brief, thorough mind exploration of the immediate vicinity of the elevator. Finally she opened the door, then swiftly shut it behind her. There was a plane less than thirty feet away. Beyond it was another plane on which three mechanics were working. A soldier was talking to them.

It took her only ten seconds to walk to the plane and climb in; and she had not picked the brains of air officers for nothing during the long years. The jets hissed, the great machine glided forward and became airborne.

"Huh," the thoughts of a mechanic came after her, "there goes the colonel again."

"Probably after another woman." That was the soldier.

"Yeah," said the second mechanic. "Trust that guy to—"

It took two hours of the swiftest southwest flying to reach the slan hide-out she had selected. Then she set the plane on robot control and watched it fly off into the east. During the days that followed, she watched hungrily for a car. It was on the fifteenth day that a long, black machine purred out of a belt of trees along the ancient roadway and came toward her. Her body tensed. Somehow, she had to get that driver to stop, overpower him, and take his car. Any hour now the secret police would be swooping down—she must get away from here, and fast. Eyes fixed on the car, she waited.

14

THE FLAT, WINTRY VASTNESS of the prairie was behind him at last. Jommy Cross turned more directly east, then south. Far south. And ran into an apparently endless series of police barricades. No effort was made to stop him, and he finally saw in the minds of several men that there was a search on for—*a slan girl.*

That hit him with staggering impact. Just for a moment, the hope was too big for his mind to accept. And yet, it couldn't be a tendrilless slan woman. Men, who could not recognize slans except by their tendrils, would only be searching for a true slan. Which meant . . . here was his dream come true.

Deliberately, he headed for the area which they had orders to surround. He found himself presently off the main highway, following a side road that wound down among tree-filled valleys, and up over tall hills. The morning had been grey, but at noon the sun came out and shone gloriously from a sky of azure blue.

His clear-cut impression of being close to the heart of the danger zone was strengthened abruptly as an outside thought touched his mind. It was a gentle pulsation yet so tremendous in its import that his brain rocked.

"Attention, slans! This is a Porgrave thought-broadcasting machine. Please turn up the side road half a mile ahead. A further message will be given later."

Jommy stiffened. Soft and insistent, the flowing thought wave of the message beat at him again, gentle as a summer rain: "Attention, slans! . . . Please turn . . ."

He drove on, tense but excited. The miracle had happened. Slans, somewhere near, many of them. Such a thought machine might have been developed by an individual, but the message somehow suggested the presence of a community, and it could be true slans—or could it?

The swift, sweet flow of his hope became a trickle as he pondered the possibility of a trap. This could easily be a device left over from an old slan settlement. There was no real danger, of course, not with this car to deflect dangerous blows and his weapons to paralyse the striking power of an enemy. But it was just as well to take into account the possibility that human beings had left a thought-broadcasting machine here as a trap, and that they were now closing in upon it in the belief that someone was hiding there. After all, it was that possibility that had brought him.

Under his guidance, the beautiful, streamlined car rolled forward. In a minute, Jommy Cross saw the pathway; it was little more than that. The abnormally long car whipped into it and along it. The pathway wound through heavily wooded areas, through several small valleys. It was three miles farther on that the next message brought him to an abrupt stop.

"This is a Porgrave broadcaster. It directs you, a true slan, to the little farm ahead, which provides entrance to an underground city of factories, gardens and residences. Welcome. This is a Porgrave—"

There was a great bouncing as the car struck a row of small ridges; and then the machine broke through a thick hedge of yielding willows and emerged into a shallow clearing. Jommy Cross found himself staring across a weed-grown yard to where a weather-beaten farmhouse drooped beside two other age-weary buildings, a barn and a garage.

Windowless, unpainted, the rickety old two-storey house gaped sightlessly at him. The barn tottered like the ancient hulk that it was; its roller door hooked on one roller only, and the other end edged deep into the forsaken soil.

His gaze flashed briefly to the garage, then away, then back again thoughtfully. There was the same appearance of something long dead—and yet it was different. The subtle difference grew on him, bringing interest in its wake. The garage seemed to totter, but it was by design, not through decay. There were hard metals here, rigidly set against the elements.

The apparently broken doors leaned heavily against the ground, yet opened lightly before the pressing fingers of the tall, lithely built young woman in a grey dress who came out and gazed at him with a dazzling smile.

She had flashing eyes, this girl, and a finely moulded, delicately textured face, and because his mind was always held on a tight band of thought, she came out thinking he was a human being.

And she was a slan!

And he was a slan!

For Jommy Cross, who had searched the world with caution for so many long years, his mind always alert, the shock and recovery from the shock were almost simultaneous. He had known that someday this would happen; that someday he would meet another slan. But for Kathleen, who had never had to conceal her thoughts, the surprise was devastating. She fought for control and found herself uncontrollable. The little-used shield was suddenly, briefly, unusable.

There was a noble pride in the rich flow of thought matter that streamed from her mind in that instant when her brain was like an open, unprotected book. Pride, and a golden humility. Humility based on a deep sensitivity, an immense understanding that equalled his own, yet lacked the tempering of unending struggle and danger. There was a warm goodheartedness in her that had nevertheless known resentment and tears, and faced limitless hate.

And then her mind closed tight, and she stood wide-eyed, looking at him. After a long moment she unlocked her mind and let a thought reach out to him:

"We mustn't stay here. I've been here too long, already. You probably saw in my mind about the police, so the best thing we can do is to drive away immediately."

He just stood there, gazing at her with shining eyes. Each passing second, his mind expanded more, his whole body felt warm with joy. It was like an intolerable weight lifting. All these years everything had depended on him. The great weapon he held in trust for that future world he sometimes dreamed of hung suspended like a monstrous sword of Damocles over the destiny of human being and slan alike by the single, fragile thread of his life. And now, there would be two life threads to control it.

It was not a thought, but an emotion; all sad, sweet, glorious emotion. A man and a woman, alone in the world, meeting like this, just as his father and mother had met long ago. He smiled reminiscently and opened his mind wide to her. He shook his head.

"No, not right away. I caught a flash from your mind about the machines in the cave city, and I would like to have a look at them. Heavy machinery is my greatest lack." He smiled reassuringly. "Don't worry too much about the danger. I have some weapons that human beings cannot match, and this car is a very special means of escape. It can go practically anywhere. I hope there is room for it in the cave."

"Oh, yes. First you go down by a series of elevators. Then you can drive anywhere. But we mustn't delay. We—"

Jommy Cross laughed happily. "No buts!" he said.

Later, Kathleen repeated her doubts: "I really don't think we ought to stay. I can see in your mind about your marvellous weapons, and that your car is made of a metal you call ten-point steel. But you also have a tendency to discount human beings. You mustn't! In their fight against slans, men like John Petty have had their brains keyed to a pitch of abnormal power. And John Petty will stop at nothing to destroy me. Even now his net must be tightening systematically around the various slan hiding places where I might be."

Jommy Cross stared at her with troubled eyes. All around was the silence of the cave city: the once white walls that pushed bravely up to the cracking ceiling, the row on row of pillars, bent and worn more from the weight of years than from the heavy earth that pressed them down. To his left he could see the beginning of the great expanse of artificial garden and the gleaming underground stream that fed water to this little subworld. To his right stretched the long row of apartment doors, the plastic walls still gleaming dully.

A people had lived here and had been driven forth by their remorseless enemies, but the menacing atmosphere of the flight seemed to linger still. Looking around, Jommy guessed that the settlement had been evacuated not less than twenty-five years before; it all still seemed very near and deadly. His thought answer to Kathleen reflected the grim threat of that lowering danger.

"By all the laws of logic, we have only to be on the alert for outside thoughts and stay within a few hundred yards of my car to be absolutely safe. Yet I'm alarmed by your intuition of danger. Please search your brain and try to discover the basis for your fear. I can't do it for you as well as you can do it for yourself."

The girl was silent. Her eyes closed. Her shield went up. She sat there beside him in the car, looking strangely like a beautiful overgrown child fallen asleep. Finally her sensitive lips twitched. For the first time she spoke aloud.

"Tell me, what is ten-point steel?"

"Ah," said Jommy Cross in satisfaction, "I'm beginning to understand the psychological factors involved. Mental communication has many advantages, but it cannot convey the extent, for instance, of a weapon's power as well as a picture on a piece of paper, or not even as well as by word of mouth. Power, size, strength and similar images do not transmit well."

"Go on."

"Everything I've done," Jommy Cross explained, "has been based on my father's great discovery of the first law of atomic energy—concentration as opposed to the old method of diffusion. So far as I know, Father never suspected the metal-strengthening possibilities, but, like all research workers who come after the great man and his basic discovery, I concentrated on details of development, based on his ideas, partly on ideas that progressively suggested themselves.

"All metals are held together by atomic tensions, which comprise the theoretical strength of that metal. In the case of steel, I called this theoretical potential one-point. As a comparison, when steel was first invented its strength was about two-thousand-point. Now processes rapidly increased this to around one-thousand, then, over a period of hundreds of years, to the present human level of seven-hundred-and-fifty.

"Tendrilless slans have made five-hundred-point steel, but even that incredibly hard stuff cannot compare with the product of my application of atomic strain, which changes the very structure of the atoms and produces the almost perfect ten-point steel. An eighth of an inch of ten-point can stop the most powerful explosive known to human beings and tendrilless slans!"

Briefly, he described his attempted trip to the Moon and the mine that sent him scurrying home, badly smashed. He concluded: "The important thing to remember there is that an atomic bomb obviously big enough to blow up a giant battleship did not penetrate a foot of ten-point, though the hull was badly dented and the engine room a shambles from transmitted shock."

Kathleen was gazing at him, her eyes shining. "What a silly fool I am," she breathed. "I've met the greatest living slan and I'm trying to fill him with the fears gathered from twenty-one years of living with human beings and their comparatively infinitesimal powers and forces."

Jommy Cross shook his head smilingly. "The great man is not me, but my father—though he had his faults, too, the biggest one being lack of adequate self-protection. But that's true genius." The smile faded. "I'm afraid, though, that we'll have to make frequent visits to this cave, and every one will be just as dangerous as this one. I have met John Petty very briefly, and what I've seen in your mind only adds to a picture of a ruthlessly thorough man. I know he's keeping a watch on this place, but really we cannot allow ourselves to be frightened by such a prospect. We'll stay only till dark this time—just long enough for me to examine the machinery. There's some food in the car that we can cook after I've had a little sleep. I'll sleep in the car, of course. But first, the machinery!"

Everywhere the big machines sprawled, like corpses, silent and mouldering. Blast furnaces, great stamping machines, lathes, saws, countless engined tools, a half-mile row on tight row of machines, about thirty per cent completely out of commission, twenty per cent partially useless, and the rest usable up to a point.

The unwinking, glareless lights made a shadowed world as they wandered along that valley of broken floor in and out among the machine hills. Jommy Cross was thoughtful.

"There's more here than I imagined—everything I have always needed. I could build a great battleship with the scrap metal alone; and they probably use it only as a means of trapping slans." His thought narrowed on her mind: "Tell me, you're sure there are only two entrances to this city?"

"There are only two entrances given on the list in Kier Gray's desk—and I've located no others."

He was silent, but he did not conceal the tenor of his thoughts from her. "Foolish of me to think again of your intuition, but I don't like to let a possible menace out of my mind till I've examined every connective probability."

"If there's a secret entrance," Kathleen volunteered, "it would take us hours to find it, and if we found one, we couldn't be sure there wouldn't be others, and so we'd feel no more secure. I still believe we should leave immediately."

Jommy Cross shook his head decisively. "I didn't let you see this in my mind before, but the main reason I don't want to leave here is that, until your face is disguised and your tendrils are hidden by false hair—a really difficult job—this is the safest place for both of us. Every highway is being watched by the police. Most of them know they're looking for a slan, and they have your picture. I turned off the main road in the hope of being able to find you before they did."

"Your machine goes up, doesn't it?" Kathleen asked.

Jommy Cross smiled mirthlessly. "Seven hours yet till dark; and every other minute we'd run into a plane. Imagine what the pilots would radio to the nearest military airport when they saw an automobile flying through the air. And if we go higher, say fifty miles, we'll surely be seen by a tendrilless slan patrol ship.

"The first commander will realize instantly who it is, report our position and attack. I've got the weapons to destroy him, but I won't be able to destroy the dozens of ships that follow—at least not before potent forces strike this car so hard that concussion alone will kill us. And besides, I cannot wilfully put myself in a position where I may have to kill anybody. I've killed only three men in my life, and every day since then my reluctance to destroy human beings has grown until now it is one of the strongest forces in me—so strong that I have based my whole plan for finding the true slans on an analysis of that one dominant trait."

The girl's thought brushed his mind, light as a breath of air. "You have a plan for finding the true slans?" she questioned.

He nodded. "Yes. It's really very simple. All the true slans I have ever met—my father, my mother, myself, and now you—have been goodhearted, kindly people. This in spite of human hatred, human efforts to destroy us. I cannot believe that we four are exceptions; and therefore there must be some reasonable explanation of all the monstrous acts which true slans seem to be committing."

He smiled briefly. "It's probably presumptuous of me even to have a thought on the subject at my age and limited development. Anyway, I'm afraid it's been an utter failure so far. And I mustn't make a major move in the game until I've taken further defensive action against the tendrilless slans."

Kathleen's eyes were fixed on him. She nodded agreement. "I can see too," she said, "why we must stay longer."

Queerly, he wished she hadn't brought up that subject again. For the barest moment (he hid the thought from her) he had a premonition of incredible danger. So incredible that logic brushed it aside. The vague backwash of it remained—made him say:

"Just stay near the car and keep your mind alert. After all, we can spot a human being a quarter of a mile away even while we're sleeping."

Oddly enough, it didn't sound the slightest bit reassuring.

At first Jommy Cross only dozed. He must have been partly awake for some minutes, because though his eyes were closed he was aware of her mind near him, and that she was reading one of his books. Once, so light was his sleep, the question came into his mind:

"The ceiling lights—do they stay on all the time?"

She must have reached softly into his brain with the answer, for suddenly he knew that the lights had been on ever since she came, and must have been like that for hundreds of years.

There was a question in her mind, and his brain answered: "No, I won't eat until I've had some sleep."

Or was that just a memory of something previously spoken?

Still he wasn't quite asleep, for a queer, glad thought welled up from deep inside him. It was wonderful to have found another slan at last, such a gorgeously beautiful girl.

And such a fine-looking young man.

Was that his thought, or hers, he wondered sleepily.

It was mine, Jommy.

What a rich joy it was to be able to entwine your mind with another sympathetic brain so intimately that the two streams of thought seemed one, and question and answer and all discussion included instantly all the subtle overtones that the cold medium of words could never transmit.

Were they in love? How could two people simply meet and be in love when, for all they knew, there were millions of slans in the world, among whom might be scores of other men and women they might have chosen under other conditions?

It's more than that, Jommy. All our lives we've been alone in a world of alien men. To find kindred at last is a special joy, and meeting all the slans in the world afterward will not be the same. We're going to share hopes and doubts, dangers and victories. Above all, we will create a child. You see, Jommy, I have already adjusted my whole being to a new way of living. Is not that true love?

He thought it was, and was conscious of great happiness. But when he slept, the happiness seemed no longer there—only a blackness that became an abyss down which he was peering into illimitable depths.

He awakened with a start. His narrowed, alert eyes flashed to where Kathleen had been sitting. The reclining chair was empty. His sharpened mind, still in the thrall of his dream, reached out.

"Kathleen!"

Kathleen came to the door of the machine. "I was looking at some of this metal, trying to imagine what would be most immediately useful to you." She stopped, smiling, and corrected herself. "To us."

Jommy Cross lay very still for a moment, reaching out with his mind, intently exploring, unhappy that she had left the car even for a moment. He divined that she came from a less tense atmosphere than himself. She had had freedom of movement and there had been, despite occasional threats, certainties that she could depend upon. In his own grim existence, an ever-present reality was that death could result from the tiniest letdown in caution. Every move had to include a calculated risk.

It was a pattern to which Kathleen would have to accustom herself. Boldness in carrying out a purpose in the face of danger was one thing. Carelessness was quite another.

Kathleen said cheerfully, "I'll make something to eat while you quickly pick out a few things you want to take along. It must be dark outside by now."

Jommy Cross glanced at his chronometer, and nodded. In two hours it would be midnight. The darkness would conceal their flight. He said slowly, "Where's the nearest kitchen?"

"Just along there." She motioned with one arm, vaguely indicating a long line of doors.

"How far?"

"About a hundred feet." She frowned. "Now, look, Jommy, I can sense how anxious you are. But if we're going to be a team, one of us has to do one thing while the other does something else."

He watched her go uneasily, wondering if the acquisition of a partner would be good for his nerves. He who had hardened himself against any danger to himself must accustom himself to the idea that she also would have to take risks.

Not that there was any danger at the moment. The hide-out was silent. Not a sound and, except for Kathleen, not a whisper of thought came from anywhere. The hunters, the searchers and the erecters of barriers that he had seen all through the day must be home by now, asleep, or about to retire.

He watched Kathleen go through a doorway, and estimated that it was nearer a hundred and fifty feet. And he was climbing out of the car when a thought came from her on a strange, high, urgent vibration:

"Jommy—the wall's opening! Somebody—"

Abruptly, her own thought broke off and she was transmitting a man's words:

"Well, if it isn't Kathleen," John Petty was saying in cold satisfaction. "And only the fifty-seventh hide-out I've visited. I've been to all of them personally, of course, because few other human beings could keep their minds from warning you of their approach. And besides, nobody could be safely trusted with such an important assignment. What do you think of the psychology of building these secret entrances to the kitchen? Apparently even slans travel on their stomachs."

Beneath Jommy Cross' swift fingers, the car leaped forward. He caught Kathleen's reply, cool and unhurried:

"So you've found me, Mr. Petty." Mockingly. "Am I, then, to beseech your mercy?"

The icy answer streamed through her mind to Jommy Cross. "Mercy is not my strong point. Nor do I delay when a long-awaited opportunity offers."

"Jommy, quick!"

The shot echoed from her mind to his. For a terrible moment of intolerable strain, her mind held off the death that the crashing bullet in her brain had brought.

"Oh, Jommy, and we could have been so happy. Good-by, my dearest—"

In a desperate dismay, he followed the life force as it faded in a flash from her mind. The black-out wall of death suddenly barred his mind from that which had been Kathleen's.

15

THERE WAS no thought in Jommy Cross, no hate, no grief, no hope—only his mind receiving impressions, and his superlatively responsive body reacting like the perfect physical machine it was. His car braked to a stop; he saw the figure of John Petty standing just beyond Kathleen's crumpled body.

"By heaven!" snapped from the surface of the man's mind, "another of them!"

His gun flashed against the impregnable armour of the car. Startled by his failure, the chief of secret police drew back. His lips parted in a cry of rage. For a moment, the dark hatred of man for the encroaching slan enemy seemed personified in his grim countenance, and in the tenseness with which his body seemed to await inevitable death.

One touch of one button, and he would have been blasted into nothingness. But Jommy Cross made no move, spoke no word. Colder, harder grew his mind as he sat there. His bleak gaze stared impersonally at the man, then at the dead body of Kathleen. And finally the measured thought came that as the sole possessor of the secret of atomic energy he could permit himself no love, no normal life. In all that world of men and slans who hated so savagely, there was for him only the relentless urgency of his high destiny.

Other men began pouring from the secret entrance, men with machine guns that chattered futilely at his car. And among them he was abruptly aware of the shields that indicated the presence of two tendrilless slans. His searching eyes spotted one of them after a moment, as the man drew into a corner, and whispered a swift message into a wrist radio. The words ran plainly along the surface of his mind:

"—a 7500 model, 200-inch base . . . general physique type 7, head 4, chin 4, mouth 3, eyes brown, type 13, eyebrows 13, nose 1, cheeks 6 . . . cut!"

He could have smashed them all, the whole venal, ghoulish crew. But no thought of vengeance could penetrate the chilled, transcendental region that was his brain. In this mad universe, there was only the safety of his weapon and the certainties that went with it.

His car backed, and raced off with a speed their legs could not match. Ahead was the tunnel of the underground creek that fed the gardens. He plunged into it, his disintegrators widening nature's crude bed for half a mile. Then he turned down to let the water stream after him and hide his tunnel, then up, so that the water wouldn't have too much space to fill.

Finally, he levelled off, and plunged on through the darkness of the underground. He couldn't head for the surface yet because the tendrilless slans would have their cruisers waiting to meet just such a possibility.

Black clouds hid a night world when at last Jommy Cross emerged from the side of a hill. He paused and, with meticulous care, undercut his tunnel, buried it under tons of crashing earth, and soared into the sky. For the second time, he clicked on his tendrilless slan radio; and this time a man's voice broke into the car:

"—Kier Gray has now arrived and taken possession of the body. It appears that once again the snake organization has allowed one of its own kind to be destroyed without a move to save her, without even the sign of a move. It is time that we drew the proper conclusions from their failures, and ceased to regard any opposition they might offer to our plans as an important factor. However, there is still the incalculable danger presented by the existence of this man Cross. It must be made clear at once that our military operations against Earth will have to be suspended until he is destroyed.

"His unexpected appearance on the scene today was, therefore, one great advantage we gained from the affair. We have a description of his car and an expert's description of his physique. No matter how he disguises himself he cannot change the bony structure of his face; and even immediate destruction of his car will not destroy the record of the car itself. There were only a few hundred thousand 7500 models sold. His will have been stolen, but it can be traced.

"Joanna Hillory, who has made a very detailed study of this snake, has been placed in charge. Under her direction, searchers will penetrate every district of every continent. There must be small areas on Earth where we have not penetrated: little valleys, stretches of prairie, particularly farming districts. Such localities must be closed, police cells set up in them.

"There is no way the snakes can contact him, for we control every avenue of communication. And from this day onward, our watchers will stop every person with his facial physique for examination.

"That will keep him off the road. That will prevent chance discovery of the snakes, and give us the time we need for our search. However long it may take, we must trace this dangerous slan to where he lives. We cannot fail. This is Great Headquarters signing off."

The rushing air whined and whistled against the hurtling car there beneath the swarming black clouds. So the war against the human world was now bound up with his own fate, an indefinite reprieve for both. They would find him, of course, these thoroughgoing slans. They had failed once before because of an unknown factor—his weapon—but that was known now; and besides, it was not a factor that would influence their remorseless search. For several minutes, he contemplated the prospective invasion of his valley, and finally emerged with one fact that remained in his favour, one question. Yes, they would find him, but how long would it take?

16

IT TOOK four years; and Jommy Cross had been twenty-three for
two months on the day when the tendrilless slan organization
struck with unexpected, unimaginable violence. He came slowly
down the veranda steps on that sultry, oppressively hot day, and
paused on the pathway that divided the garden. He was thinking
with a quiet, gentle thought of Kathleen, and of his long-dead
mother and father. It was not grief or even sadness that swayed
him, but a deep, philosophical sense of the profound tragedy
of life.

But no introspection could dull his senses. With abnormal,
unhuman clarity he was aware of his surroundings. Of all the
developments in himself during those four years, it was this
perception of *anything* that marked his growth toward maturity.
Nothing escaped him. Heat waves danced against the lower
reaches of the mountain twenty miles away, where his spaceship
was hidden. But no heat mist could bar a vision that saw so
many more pictures per split second than the human eye could
see. Details penetrated, a hard bright pattern formed where a
few years before there would have been, even for himself, a blur.

A squadron of midges swarmed past Granny, where she knelt
by a flower bed. The faint life wave of the tiny flies caressed the
supersensitive receptors of his brain. As he stood there, sound
from remoteness whispered into his ears. Wisps of thought,
shadowed by distance, touched his mind. And gradually, in
spite of incredible complexity, a kaleidoscope of the life of his
valley grew in his mind, a very symphony of impressions that
rounded beautifully into a coherent whole.

Men and women at work, children at play, laughter; tractors
moving, trucks, cars—a little farm community meeting another
day in the old, old fashion. He stared again at Granny. Briefly,
his mind dissolved into her defenceless brain, and in that
instant, so utter was his power of receiving thoughts, it was as if
she were another part of his body. A crystal-clear picture of the
dark earth she was looking at flashed from her mind to his. A
tall flower, directly under her gaze, loomed big in her mind, and
in his. As he watched, her hand came into view, holding a small,
black bug. Triumphantly, she squashed the insect, then com-
placently wiped her stained fingers in the dirt.

"Granny!" Cross said, "can't you suppress your murderous
instincts?"

The old lady glanced up at him, and there was a belligerent thrust in her wrinkled, kindly face that was reminiscent of the old Granny.

"Nonsense!" she snapped. "For ninety years now, I've killed the little devils, and my mother before me had it in for 'em too, heh, heh!"

Her giggle sounded senile. Cross frowned faintly. Granny had thrived physically in this West Coast climate, but he was not satisfied with his hypnotic reconstruction of her mind. She was very old, of course, but her constant use of certain phrases, such as the one about what she, and her mother before her, had done, was too mechanical. He had impressed the idea upon her in the first place to fill the enormous gap left by the uprooting of her own memories, but one of these days he'd have to try again. He started to turn away; and it was at that moment that the warning tingled into his brain, a sharp pulsing of faraway outside thoughts. "Airplanes!" people were thinking. "So many planes!"

It was years now since Jommy Cross had implanted the hypnotic suggestion that everybody who saw anything unusual in the valley was to signal through their subconscious, without themselves being aware of the act. The fruits of that precaution came now in the wave after wave of warning from dozens of minds.

And then he saw the planes, specks diving over the mountain heading in his general direction. Like a striking mongoose, his mind lashed out toward them, reaching for the minds of the pilots. Taut-held brain shields of tendrilless slans met that one, searching glance. In full racing stride he snatched Granny from the ground; and then he was in the house. The ten-point steel door of that ten-point steel house swung shut—even as a great, glistening, jet-propelled troop carrier plane settled like a gigantic bird among the flowers of Granny's garden.

Cross thought tensely: "A plane in every farmyard. That means they don't know exactly which one I'm in. But now the spaceships will arrive to finish the job. Thorough!"

Well, so had he been thorough, and it was obvious, now that his hand was forced, that he must push his own plan to the limit. He felt supremely confident, and there was still not a doubt in him.

Doubt and dismay came a minute later, as he stared into his underground visiplate. The battleships and cruisers were there all right, but something else, too—another ship. *A ship!* The monster filled half the visiplate, and its wheel-shaped bulk sprawled across the lower quarter of the sky. A half-mile circle of ship, ten million tons of metal, floating down lighter than air, like a buoyant flattened balloon, gigantic, immeasurably malignant in its sheer threat of unlimited power.

It came alive! A hundred-yard beam of white fire flared from its massive wall—and the solid top of the mountain dissolved before that frightful thrust. His mountain, where his ship, his life, was hidden, destroyed by *controlled atomic energy*.

Cross stood quite still there on the rug that covered the steel floor of that steel laboratory. Wisps of human incoherency from every direction fumbled at his brain. He flung up his mind shield, and that distracting confusion of outside thought was cut off abruptly. Behind him, Granny moaned in gentle terror. In the distance above him, sledge-hammer blows were lashing at his almost impregnable cottage, but the dim bedlam of noise failed to touch him. He was alone in a world of personal silence, a world of swift, quiet, uninterrupted thought.

If they were prepared to use atomic energy, why hadn't they pulverized him with bombs? A thousand co-ordinating thoughts leaped up to form the simple answer. They wanted his perfect type of atomic energy. Their method was not a development of the rather superb, so-called hydrogen bomb of old times, with its heavy water and uranium base, and chain reaction. They had gone back to an even earlier stage, a crude expansion of the cyclotron principle. That alone could explain so much size. Here was a ten-million-ton cyclotron, capable of a wild and deadly spray of energy—and they undoubtedly hoped to use its mobility to force him to give them his priceless secret.

He whirled toward the instrument board that spread across the entire end of the laboratory. A switch clicked. Pointers set rigid. And dancing needles told the story of a spaceship out there under that dissolving mountain, a ship shuddering with mechanical life, now automatically burrowing deeper into the ground, and at the same time heading unerringly toward this laboratory.

A dial spun, and a whole bank of needles in their transparent cases danced from zero to the first fractional point, and wavered there. They, also told a story—the story of atomic projectors rearing up from the ground where they had been hidden so long—and as he grasped the precision instrument that was his aiming device, twenty invincible guns out there swung in perfect synchronization.

The hairline sights edged along the unmissable spread of the ship's bulk. And paused. What was his purpose against these ruthless enemies? He didn't want to bring that monster machine to earth. He didn't want to create a situation where slans and human beings might launch into a furious struggle for the possession of the wreck. There was no doubt that the human beings would fight with a fearless ferocity. Their great mobile guns could still hurl shells capable of piercing any metal in the possession of the slans. And if any of those ships with their superior armaments ever fell into human hands, then it would be no time at all before they, also, had spaceships; and the devil's war would be on. No, he didn't want that.

And he didn't want to destroy the ship because he didn't want to kill the tendrilless slans who were in it. For, after all, tendrilless slans *did* represent a law and order which he respected. And because they were a great race, and definitely kin to him, they merited mercy.

Before that clarification, hesitation fled. Straight at the centre of that immense cyclotron, Cross aimed his battery of synchronized weapons. His thumb pressed down the fire button. Above him, the half mile of spiral-shaped ship recoiled like an elephant struck an intolerable blow. It rocked madly, like a ship in stormy seas. And briefly, as it swung sickeningly, he saw blue sky through a gaping hole—and realized his victory.

He had cut that vast spiral from end to end. In every turn of it now was a hopelessly diffusing leak. No stream of atoms, however accelerated, could run that gauntlet unmutilated. The power of the cyclotron was smashed. But all the implications of that ship remained. Frowning, Cross watched the ship poise for a moment, shakily. Slowly it began to recede, its antigravity plates apparently full on. Up, up it mounted, growing smaller as it withdrew into the distance.

At fifty miles it was still bigger than the battleships that were nosing down toward that green, almost unharmed valley. And now the implications were clearer, colder, deadlier. The nature of their attack showed that they must have spotted his activities in this valley months ago.

Clearly, they had waited until they could approach in one titanic, organized battle, with the purpose of forcing him out where they could follow him night and day by means of their instruments and so, by sheer weight of numbers and guns, destroy him and capture his equipment.

Dispassionately, Cross turned to Granny. "I'm going to leave you here. Follow my instructions to the letter. Five minutes from now, you will go up the way we came down, closing all the metal doors behind you. You will then forget all about this laboratory. It is going to be destroyed, so you might as well forget. If men question you, you will act senile, but at other times you will be normal. I'm leaving you to face that danger because I'm no longer sure, in spite of my precautions, that I can come out of this alive."

He felt a chill, impersonal interest in the knowledge that the day of action had arrived. The tendrilless slans might intend this attack on him to be but part of a vaster design that included their long-delayed assault on Earth. Whatever happened, his plans were as complete as he could make them; and though it was years too soon, he must now force the issue to the limit of his power. He was on the run, and there could be no turning back—for behind him was swift death!

Cross' ship nosed out of the little river and launched toward space on a long, slanting climb. It was important that he should not become invisible until the slans actually saw that he was out of the valley, before they had razed it in futile search. But first, there was one thing he must do.

His hand plunged home a switch. His narrowed gaze fastened on the rear visiplate, which showed the valley falling away below. At a score of points on that green floor (he counted them in lightning calculation) white flame blazed up in a strange, splotchy-looking fire. Down there, every weapon, every atomic machine, was turning on itself. Fire chambers were burning out, metal running molten in that devouring violence of energy.

The white glow was still there as he turned away a few seconds later, grimly content. Now let them search through that ravaged, twisted metal. Let their scientists labour to bring to life a secret they craved so desperately, and to obtain which they had come out where human beings could see some of their powers. In every burned-out cache in that valley, they would find exactly nothing!

The destruction of all that was so precious to the attackers required a fraction of a minute, but in that time he was seen. Four dead-black battleships turned toward him simultaneously —and then hovered uncertainly as he actuated the mechanism that made his vessel invisible.

Abruptly, their possession of atom-energy detectors was shown. The ships fell in behind him unerringly. Alarm bells showed others ahead, closing toward him. It was only the unmatchable atomic drivers that saved him from that vast fleet. There were so many vessels that he could not even begin to count them, and all that could come near turned their deadly projectors where their instruments pointed. They missed, because during the very instant they spotted him, his machine flashed out of range of their most massive guns.

Completely invisible, travelling at many miles per second, his ship headed for Mars! He must have hurtled through mine fields, but that didn't matter now. The devouring disintegration rays that poured out from the walls of his great machine ate up mines before they could explode, and simultaneously destroyed every light-wave that would have revealed his craft to alert eyes out there in the blaze of Sun.

There was only one difference. The mines were smashed *before* they reached his ship. Light, being in a wave state as it flashed up, could be destroyed only during that fraction of instant when it touched his ship and started to bounce. At the very moment of bouncing, its speed reduced, the corpuscles that basically composed it lengthened according to the laws of the Lorentz-FitzGerald contraction theory—at that instant of almost quiescence, the fury of the Sun's rays was blotted out by the disintegrators.

And, because light must touch the walls first, and so could be absorbed as readily as ever, his visiplates were unaffected. The full picture of everything came through even as he hurtled on, unseen, invisible. His ship seemed to stand still in the void, except that gradually Mars became larger. At a million miles, it was a great, glowing ball as big as the Moon seen from Earth; and it grew like an expanding balloon until its dark bulk filled half the sky, and lost its redness.

Continents took form, mountains, seas, incredible gorges, rock-strewn and barren stretches of flat land. Grimmer grew the picture, deadlier every forsaken aspect of that gnarled old planet. Mars, seen through an electric telescope at thirty thousand miles, was like a too-old human being, withered, bony, ugly, cold-looking, drooling with age, enormously repellent.

The dark area that was Mare Cimmerium showed as a fanged, terrible sea. Silent, almost tideless, the waters lay under the eternal blue-dark skies; but no ship could ever breast those placid waters. Endless miles of jagged rocks broke the surface. There were no patterns, no channels, simply the sea and the protruding rock. Finally, Cross saw the city, making a strange, shimmering picture under its vast roof of glass; then a second city showed, and a third.

Far, far past Mars he plunged, his motors dead, not the tiniest amount of atomic energy diffusing from any part of his ship. That was caution, pure and simple. There could be no fear of detector intruments in these vast distances. At last, the gravitational field of the planet began to check his flight. Slowly, the long machine yielded to the inexorable pull and began to fall toward the night side of the globe. It was a slow task. Earth days fled into Earth weeks. But finally he turned on, not his atomic energy, but the antigravity plates which he had not used since he had installed his atomic drives.

For days and days then, while centrifugal action of the planet cushioned his swift fall, he sat without sleep, staring into the visiplates. Five times the ugly balls of dark metal that were mines flashed toward him. Each time he actuated for brief seconds his all-devouring wall disintegrators—and waited for the ships that might have spotted his momentary use of force. A dozen times, his alarm bells clanged, and lights flashed on his visiplates, but no ships came within range. Below him, the planet grew vast, and filled every horizon with its dark immensity. There were not many landmarks on this night portion aside from the cities. Here and there, however, splashes of light showed some kind of habitation and activity, and at last he found what he wanted. A mere dot of flame, like a candle fluttering in remote darkness.

It turned out to be a small mine, and the light came from the little house where the four tendrilless slans who attended the mine's completely automatic machinery lived. It was almost dark before Cross returned to his ship, satisfied that this was what he wanted.

A mist of blackness lay like a black cloth over the planet the following night when, once again, Cross landed his ship in the ravine that led toward the mine head. Not a shadow stirred. Not a sound invaded the silence as he edged forward to the mouth of the mine. Gingerly, he took out one of the metal cases which protected his hypnotism crystals, inserted the atomically unstable, glasslike object into a crack of the rock entrance—jerked off the protective covering and raced off before his own body could affect the sluggish thing. In the black of the ravine, he waited.

In twenty minutes, a door of the cottage opened. The flood of light from within revealed the outlines of a tall young man. Then the door closed; a torch blazed in the hand of the shadowed figure, glared along the path he was following, and brought a flash of reflected flame from the hypnotism crystal. The man walked toward it curiously, and stooped to examine it. His thoughts ran along the surface of his casually protected mind.

"Funny! That crystal wasn't there this morning." He shrugged. "Some rock probably jarred loose, and the crystal was behind it."

He stared at it, abruptly startled by its fascination. Suspicion leaped into his alert mind. He pondered the thing with a cold, tense logic. And dived for the shelter of the cavern as Cross' paralysing ray flicked at him from the ravine. He fell unconscious just inside the cave.

Cross rushed forward, and in a few minutes had the man far down the ravine, out of all possible earshot of the mine. But even during those first minutes, his mind was reaching through the other's shattered mind shield, searching. It was slow work, because moving around in an unconscious mind was like walking under water, there was so much resistance. But suddenly, he found what he was seeking, the corridor made by the man's sharp awareness of the pattern of the crystal.

Swiftly, Cross followed the mind path to its remote end in the complex root-sources of the brain. A thousand paths streamed loosely before him, scattering in every direction. Grimly, with careful yet desperate speed, he followed them, ignoring the obviously impossible ones. And then, once more, like a burglar who opens safes by listening for the faint click that reveals he has reached another stage in the solution of the combination, once more a key corridor stretched before him.

Eight key paths, fifteen minutes, and the combination was his, the brain was his. Under his ministrations the man, whose name was Miller, revived with a gasp. Instantly, he closed the shield tight over his mind.

Cross said, "Don't be so illogical. Lower your shield."

The shield went down; and in the darkness the surprised tendrilless slan stared at him, astonishment flaming through his mind.

"Hypnotized, by heaven!" he said wonderingly. "How the devil did you do it?"

"The method can be used only by true slans," Cross replied coolly, "so explanations would be useless."

"A true slan!" the other said slowly. "Then you're Cross!"

"I'm Cross."

"I suppose you know what you're doing," Miller went on, "but I don't see how you expect to gain anything by your control of me."

Abruptly, Miller's mind realized the strangeness, the eeriness of the conversation there in that dark ravine, under the black, mist-hidden sky. Only one of the two moons of Mars was visible, a blurred, white shape that gleamed remotely from the vast vault of heaven. He said quickly:

"How is it that I can talk to you, reason with you? I thought hypnotism was a mind-dulling thing."

"Hypnotism," Cross cut in without pausing in his swift exploration of the other's brain, "is a science that involves many factors. Full control permits the subject apparently complete freedom, except that his will is under absolute outside domination. But there is no time to waste." His voice grew sharper, and his brain withdrew from the other. "Tomorrow is your day off. You will go to the Bureau of Statistics and ascertain the name and present location of every man with my physical structure."

He stopped, because Miller was laughing softly. His mind and voice said, "Good heavens, man, I can tell you that right now. They were all spotted after your description came through several years ago. They're always under observation; they're all married men and—" His voice trailed off.

Sardonically, Cross said, "Go on!"

Miller went on, reluctantly. "There are twenty-seven men, all together, who resemble you in very great detail, a surprisingly high average."

"Go on!"

"One of them," said Miller disconsolately, "is married to a woman whose head was badly injured in a spaceship accident

128

last week. They're building up her brain and bone again, but—"

"But that will take a few weeks," Cross finished for him. "The man's name is Barton Corliss. He's located at the Cimmerium spaceship factory and, like yourself, goes into the city Cimmerium every fourth day."

"There ought to be an enforceable law," Miller said glumly, "against people who can read minds. Fortunately, the Porgrave receivers will spot you," he finished more cheerfully.

"Eh?" Cross spoke sharply. He had already noticed about mind reading in Miller's mind, but it had not seemed applicable. And there had been other, more important things to follow up.

Coolly, Miller said, and his thoughts verified every word of it: "The Porgrave broadcaster broadcasts thoughts, and the Porgrave receiver receives them. In Cimmerium, there's one located every few feet; they're in all the buildings, houses, everywhere. They're our protection against snake spies. One indiscreet thought, and finish!"

Cross was silent. At last he said, "One more question, and I want your mind to give off a lot of thoughts on this. I want detail."

"Yes?"

"How imminent is the attack on Earth?"

"It has been decided," Miller replied precisely, "that in view of the failure to destroy you and obtain your secret, control of Earth has become essential, the purpose being to forestall any future danger from anybody. To this end vast reserves of spaceships are being turned out; the fleet is mobilizing at key points, but the date of attack, though probably decided on, has not yet been announced."

"What have they planned to do with human beings?"

"To hell with human beings!" Miller said coolly. "When our own existence is involved, we can't worry about them."

The darkness all around seemed deeper, the chill of the night beginning to penetrate even his heated clothes. Instant by instant, Cross' mind grew harder as he examined the implications of Miller's words. War! In a bleak voice, he said:

"Only with the help of the true slans can that attack be stopped. I must find them—somewhere—and I've exhausted most of the possibilities. I am now going to the most likely remaining place."

The morning dragged. The sun gleamed like a festering sore in the blue-black vastness of the sky. And the sharp, black shadows that it cast on the land grew narrow, and then began to lengthen again as Mars turned an unfriendly afternoon face to the insistent light.

From where Cross' ship crouched in the great chalk cliff, the horizon was a thing of blurred ridges against the shadowed sky. But even from his two-thousand-foot height, the nearness of the horizon was markedly noticeable. Twilight threatened, and then at last his patient vigil was rewarded. The small, red-striped, torpedo-shaped object drifted up from the horizon, fire pouring from its rear. The rays of the sinking sun glinted on its dull, metallic skin. It darted far to the left of where Cross waited in his machine, that like some beast of prey, lay entunnelled in the swelling breast of the white cliff.

About three miles, Cross estimated carefully. The actual bulk of the intervening distance would make no difference to the motor that lay silent in the engine room in the back of the ship, ready to give forth its noiseless, stupendous power.

Three hundred miles, and that superb motor would vibrate on without strain, without missing a single beat—except that such titanic force could not be unleashed where its strength might touch ground, and tear a swath out of this already tortured land.

Three miles, four, five—he made swift adjustments. Then the force of the magnetors flashed across the miles and, simultaneously, the idea he had developed during his long trip from Earth took life from a special engine. Radio waves, so similar to the vibrations of energy he was using that only an extremely sensitive instrument could have detected the difference, sprayed forth from a robot motor that he had set up five hundred miles away. For those brief minutes, the whole planet sighed with energy waves.

Out there somewhere tendrilless slans must already be plotting the centre of that interfering wave. Meantime, his small use of power should go unnoticed. Swiftly, yet gently, the magnetors did their work. The faraway, still receding ship slowed as if it had run into resistance. It slowed—and then was drawn inexorably back toward the chalk cliff.

Effortlessly, using the radio waves as a screen for further use of power, Cross withdrew his own ship deeper into the cliff's bulging belly, widening the natural tunnel with a spray of dissolving energy. Then, like a spider with a fly, he pulled the smaller machine into the lair after him.

In a moment a door opened, and a man appeared. He leaped lightly to the tunnel floor, and stood for a moment peering against the glare of the searchlight of the other ship. With easy confidence, he walked closer. His eyes caught the gleam of the crystal in the dank wall of the cave.

He glanced at it casually, then the very abnormality of a thing that could distract his attention at such a moment penetrated to his consciousness. As he plucked it out of the wall, Cross' paralysing ray sent him sprawling.

Instantly, Cross clicked off all power. A switch closed; and the distant robot atomic-wave broadcaster dissolved in the fire of its own energy.

As for the man, all Cross wanted from him this time was a full-length photograph, a record of his voice, and hypnotic control. It took only twenty minutes before Corliss was flying off again toward Cimmerium, inwardly raging against his enslavement, outwardly unable to do anything about it.

There could be no hurrying of what Cross knew he must do before he could dare enter Cimmerium. Everything had to be anticipated, an almost unlimited amount of detail painstakingly worked out. Every fourth day—his holiday—Corliss called at the cave, coming and going, and as the urgent weeks passed, his mind was drained of memory, of detail. Finally, Cross was ready, and the next, the seventh holiday, his plans came to life. One Barton Corliss remained in the cave, deep in hypnotic sleep; the other one climbed into the small, red-striped craft and sped toward the city of Cimmerium.

It was twenty minutes later that the battleship flashed down from the sky, and loomed up beside him, a vast mass of streamlined metal ship.

"Corliss," said a man's clipped voice in the ship's radio, "in the course of normal observation of all slans resembling the snake, Jommy Cross, we waited for you at this point, and find that you are approximately five minutes overdue.

"You will accordingly proceed to Cimmerium under escort, where you will be taken before the military commission for examination. That is all."

17

CATASTROPHE CAME as simply as that. An accident not altogether unexpected, but bitterly disappointing nonetheless. Six times before, Barton Corliss had been as much as twenty minutes overdue; and it had gone undetected. Now, five minutes of equally unavoidable delay—and the long arm of chance had struck at the hope of a world.

Gloomily, Cross stared into the visiplates. Below him was rock. Rock seamed and gnarled and unutterably deserted. No longer were the ravines like small arroyos. They slashed in all directions like a wild beast at bay. Vast valleys snarled into life; gorges sheered off into unplumbable depths, and then leaped up ferociously in ugly snags of mountain. This trackless waste was his way out, if ever he desired to escape, for no captured ship, however large and formidable, could hope to run the gauntlet that the tendrilless slans could throw up between himself and his own indestructible machine.

Some hope still remained, of course. He had an atomic revolver, which was built to resemble Corliss' gun and which actually fired an electric charge, until the secret mechanism for the atomic energy blast was activated. And the wedding ring on his finger was as near a copy as he could make of the one that Corliss wore, the great difference being that it contained the smallest atomic generator ever constructed, and was designed, like the gun, to dissolve if tampered with. Two weapons and a dozen crystals—to stop the war of wars!

The land that fled beneath his prison ship grew wilder now. Black, placid water began to show in oily, dirty streaks at the bottom of those primeval abysses, the beginning of the unclean, unbeautiful sea that was Mare Cimmerium.

Abruptly, there was unnatural life! On a tableland of mountain to his right a cruiser lay like a great, browsing black shark. A swarm of hundred-foot gunboats lay motionless on the rock around it, a wicked-looking school of deep-space fish that partly hid the even deadlier reality of the land on which their hard bellies rested. Before his penetrating vision, the mountain became a design of steel and stone fortress. Black steel, cleverly woven into black rock; gigantic guns peering into the sky.

And there, to the left this time, was another tableland of steel and time-tempered rock, another cruiser and its complement of pilot ships lying heavily in their almost invisible cradles. The guns grew thicker; and always they pointed skyward, as if waiting tensely for some momentarily expected and monstrously dangerous enemy. So much defence, so incredibly much *offence*, against what? Could these tendrilless slans be so uncertain about the true slans that even all these potent weapons could not quench their fear of those elusive beings?

A hundred miles of forts and guns and ships! A hundred miles of impassable gorge and water and frightful, upjutting cliffs. And then his ship and the great armoured vessel that was his escort soared over a spreading peak; and there in the near distance glittered the glass city of Cimmerium. And the hour of his examination had come.

The city rode high on a plain that shrank back from the sheer-falling, ragged edge of a solid, dark tongue of sea. The glass flashed in the sun, a burning white fire that darted over the surface in vivid bursts of flame. It was not a big city. But it was as big as it could be in that forbidding area of land. It crowded with tightfitting temerity to the very edge of the gorges that ringed its glass roof. Its widest diameter was three miles; at its narrowest point, it sprawled a generous two miles; and in its confines dwelt two hundred thousand slans, according to the figures he had obtained from Miller and Corliss.

The landing field was where he had expected it would be. It was a flat expanse of metal at one projecting edge of the city, big enough to take a battleship, and it was streaked with shining threads of railway. Lightly, his small machine settled toward one of the tracks onto metal cradle Number 9977. Simultaneously, the great bulk of warship above him surged off toward the sea, and was instantly lost to sight as it passed the towering cliff edge of glasslike roof.

Below him, the automatic machinery of the cradle rolled on its twin rails toward a great steel door. The door opened automatically, and shut behind him.

What his swift vision beheld in that first moment of entry was not unexpected, but the reality soared beyond the picture of it that he had seen in the minds of Miller and Corliss. There must have been a thousand ships in the section of the vast hangar that he could see. From roof to ceiling, they were packed in like sardines in a can, each in its cradle; and each, he knew, capable of being called forth if the proper numbers were punched on the section instrument board.

The machine stopped. Cross climbed casually down and nodded curtly to the three slans who waited there for him. The oldest of the three came forward, smiling faintly.

"Well, Barton, so you've earned another examination! You may be sure of a swift, thorough job—the usual, of course:

133

fingerprinting, X-ray, blood test, chemical reaction of the skin, microscope measurement of hair, and so on."

There was expectancy in the overtone of thought that leaked from the minds of the three men. But Cross did not need their thoughts. He had never been more alert, his brain had never been clearer, never more capable of distinguishing the subtlest exactness of details. He said mildly:

"Since when has chemical reaction of the skin been a usual part of the examination?"

The men did not apologize for their little trap, nor did their thoughts show any disappointment at failure. And Cross felt no thrill at this first small victory. For no matter what happened at this early stage, he could not possibly stand a thorough examination. He must use to the limit the preparations he had made these last several weeks when he had analysed the information from Miller's and Corliss' minds.

The youngest man said, "Bring him into the laboratory and we'll get the physical part of this examination over. Take his gun, Prentice."

Cross handed over the weapon without a word.

They waited then, the oldest man, Ingraham, smiling expectantly, Bradshaw, the youngest, staring at him with unwinking grey eyes. Prentice alone looked indifferent as he pocketed Cross' gun. But it was the silence, not their actions, that caught Cross' mind. There was not a physical sound, nowhere even a whisper of conversation. The whole community of the hangar was like a graveyard, and for the moment it seemed impossible that beyond those walls a city hummed with activity in preparation for war.

He actuated the combination, and watched his cradle and ship slide off soundlessly, first horizontally, then up toward the remote ceiling. There was abruptly the faintest squealing of metal, and then it settled into position. And silence grew again over the brief protrusion of sound.

Smiling inwardly at the way they were watching him for the slightest error of procedure, Cross led the way to the exit. It opened onto a shining corridor, the smooth walls of which were spaced at intervals with closed doors. When they were within sight of the entrance to the laboratory, Cross said:

"I suppose you called the hospital in time, telling them I would be delayed."

Ingraham stopped short, and the others followed suit. They stared at him. Ingraham said, "Good heavens, is your wife being revived this morning?"

Unsmiling, Cross nodded. "The doctors were to have her on the verge of consciousness twenty minutes after I was due to land. At that time they will have been working for approximately an hour. Your examination and that of the military commission will obviously have to be postponed."

There was no disagreement. Ingraham said, "The military will escort you, no doubt."

It was Bradshaw who spoke briefly into his wrist radio. The tiny, yet clear, answer reached to Cross.

"Under ordinary circumstances, the military patrol would escort him to the hospital. But it happens that we are confronted by the most dangerous individual the world has ever known. Cross is only twenty-three, but it is a proven fact that danger and adversity mature men and slans at an early age. We can assume, then, that we are dealing with a full-grown true slan, possessed of weapons and powers of unknown potentialities.

"If Corliss should actually be Cross, then the coincidence of Mrs. Corliss' return to consciousness at this important hour betokens preparation for all possible contingencies, particularly of suspicion at the moment of landing. He had already suffered a setback in that there is going to be an examination.

"Nevertheless, the very fact that postponement has been necessitated for the first time in our examination of men resembling Cross requires that experts trained in preliminary examination be with him every second of the time. You will, therefore, carry on until further orders. A surface car is waiting at the head of elevator Number I."

As they emerged into the street, Bradshaw said, "If he is not Corliss, then he will be absolutely useless at the hospital and Mrs. Corliss' mind will possibly be permanently injured."

Ingraham shook his head. "You're mistaken. True slans can read minds. He'll be able to do as good a job of sensing errors in the surgical room as Corliss with the aid of the Porgrave receivers."

Cross caught the grim smile on Bradshaw's face as the slan said softly, "Your voice trailed off there, Ingraham. Did it suddenly occur to you that the presence of the Porgraves will prevent Cross from using his mind, except in the most limited way?"

"Another thing"—it was Prentice who spoke—"the reason for Corliss' going to the hospital at all is that he will recognize when something is wrong because of the natural affinity between a husband and wife. But that also means that Mrs. Corliss will recognize instantly whether or not he is her husband."

Ingraham was smiling grimly. "We have, then, the final conclusion: If Corliss is Cross the revival of Mrs. Corliss in his presence may have tragic results for her. Those very results will go far to prove his identity, even if all other tests we make turn out negatively."

Cross said nothing. He had made a thorough examination of

the problem presented by the Porgrave receivers. They constituted a danger, but they were only machines. His control over his mind should reduce that menace.

Recognition by Mrs. Corliss was another matter. Affinity between a sensitive husband and his sensitive wife was easily understandable, and it was unthinkable that he should contribute to the destruction of this slan woman's mind. Somehow he must save her sanity, but save himself, also.

The car sped smoothly along a boulevard that glowed with flowers. The road was dark, glassy in appearance, and not straight. It wound in and out among the tall, spreading trees that half hid the buildings that lined the far sides of the shaded walks to the left and right. The buildings were low-built structures, and their beauty, the flowing artistry of their design, surprised him. He had captured something of the picture they made from the minds of Miller and Corliss, but this triumph of architectural genius was beyond his anticipation. A fortress was not expected to be beautiful; gun turrets ordinarily were for usefulness rather than to serve as poems of architecture.

As it was, they served their purpose admirably. They looked like actual buildings, part of an actual city, instead of being merely a thick armoured screen for the true city below. Once again the vastness of the defence forces showed with what respect the true slans were viewed. A world of men was going to be attacked because of the tendrilless slan fear, and that was the ultimate in tragic irony.

"If I'm right," Cross thought, "and the true slans are living in with the tendrilless slans, as the tendrilless slans in their turn live with the human beings, then all this preparation is against an enemy that has already slipped inside the defences."

The car stopped in an alcove that led to an elevator. The elevator dropped as swiftly into the depths as the first elevator had come up out of the hangar. Casually, Cross took one of the metal "crystal" cubes out of his pocket and tossed it into the wastepaper receptacle that fitted snugly into one corner of the cage. He saw that the slan had followed his action. He explained:

"Got a dozen of those things, but apparently eleven is all I can comfortably carry. The weight of the others kept pressing that one against my side."

It was Ingraham who stooped and picked up the little thing. "What is it?"

"The reason for my delay. I'll explain to the commission later. The twelve are all exactly the same, so that one won't matter."

Ingraham stared at it thoughtfully, and was just about to open it when the elevator stopped. He put it decisively into his pocket. "I'll keep this," he said. "You go out first, Corliss."

Without hesitation, Cross stepped into the broad marble

corridor. A woman in a white cloak came forward. "You'll be called in a few minutes, Barton. Wait here."

She vanished into a doorway, and Cross grew aware of a surface thought from Ingraham. He turned as the older slan spoke.

"This business of Mrs. Corliss worries me so much that I feel that before we allow you in there, Corliss, we ought to make a simple test that we haven't used for years because of its lack of dignity, and because of other equally effective tests."

"What's the test?" Cross asked curtly.

"Well, if you're Cross, you'll be wearing false hair to cover your slan tendrils. If you're Corliss, the natural strength of your hair would enable us to lift you right off the ground, and you'd scarcely feel it. False hair, artificially fastened on, could not possibly stand pressure. So, for the sake of your wife, I'm going to ask you to bend your head. We'll be gentle, and apply the pressure gradually."

Cross smiled. "Go ahead! I think you'll find that it's genuine hair."

It was, of course. Long since, he had discovered a kind of answer to that problem—a thick fluid that, worked over the roots of his hair, gradually hardened into a thin layer of rubbery, fleshy-looking stuff, sufficient to cover his betraying tendrils. By carefully twisting the hair just before the hardening process was completed, tiny air holes were formed through to the hair roots.

Frequent removal of the material, and long periods of leaving his hair and head in the natural state, had in the past proved sufficient to keep the health of his head unimpaired. Something similar, it seemed to him, was what the true slans must have been doing these many years. The danger lay in the periods of "rest."

Ingraham said finally, grudgingly, "It doesn't really prove anything. If Cross ever comes here, he won't be caught on anything as simple as that. Here's the doctor, and I guess it's all right."

The bedroom was large and grey and full of softly pulsing machines. The patient was not visible, but there was a long metal case, like a streamlined coffin, one end of which pointed toward the door; the other end Cross couldn't see, but he knew the woman's head was projecting from that far side.

Attached to the top of the case was a bulging, transparent test tube affair. Pipes ran from it down into the "coffin," and through these pipes, through that bulbous bottle, flowed a rich, steady stream of red blood. A solid bank of instruments sat just beyond the woman's protuding head. Lights were there, glowing with the faintest unsteadiness, as if now one, now another was yielding obstinately to some hidden pressure. Each time, the one affected fought stubbornly to regain the infinitesimal loss of brightness.

From where the doctor made him stop, Cross could see the woman's head against the background of those whispering machines. No, not her head. Only the bandages that completely swathed her head were visible; and it was into the white pulp of bandage that the host of wires from the instrument board disappeared.

Her mind was unshielded, a still-broken thing, and it was into the region of semi-thoughts that flowed along in dead-slow time that Cross probed cautiously.

He knew the theory of what the tendrilless slan surgeons had done. The body was entirely disconnected from nervous contact with the brain by a simple system of short circuit. The brain itself, kept alive by rapid tissue-building rays, had been divided into twenty-seven sections; and, thus simplified, the enormous amount of repair work had been swiftly performed.

His thought wave sped past those operation "breaks" and "mends." There were faults in plenty, he saw, but all of a distinctly minor character, so superbly had the surgical work been done. Every section of that powerful brain would yield to the healing force of the tissue-building rays. Beyond doubt, Mrs. Corliss would open her eyes a sane, capable young woman, and recognize him for the imposter he was.

In spite of urgency, Cross thought, "I was able to hypnotize human beings without the aid of crystals years ago, though it took a great deal longer. Why not slans?"

She was unconscious, and her shield down. At first, he was too aware of the Porgrave receivers, and the danger they offered. And then he grooved his mind to the anxiety vibration that would be normal for Corliss regardless of the circumstances. All fear drained from his brain. He strained forward with frantic speed.

It was the method of the operation that saved him. A properly knit slan brain would have required hours to explore, without a clue to the proper beginning. But now, in this mind split by master surgeons into its twenty-seven natural compartments, the mass of cells comprising the will power was easily recognizable. In one minute he was at the control centre, and the palpable force of his thought waves had gained him control.

He had time then to place the earphones of the Porgrave receivers over his head, noting at the same time that Bradshaw already had on a pair—for him, he thought grimly. But there was no suspicion at the surface of the young slan's mind. Evidently, thought in the form of an almost pure physical force, completely pictureless, could not be translated by the Porgraves. His own tests were confirmed.

The woman stirred mentally and physically and the incoherent

thought in her mind clattered as a sound in his earphones:
"Fight . . . occupation—"

The words fitted only because she had been a military commander, but there was not enough to make sense. Silence, then:

"June . . . definitely June . . . be able to clear up before winter then, and have no unnecessary deaths from cold and dislocation . . . that's settled, then . . . June 10th—"

He could have repaired the faults in her brain in ten minutes by hypnotic suggestion. But it took an hour and a quarter of cautious co-operation with the surgeons and their vibration-pressure machine, and almost every minute of the time he was thinking about her words.

So June 10th was the day of the attack on Earth. This was April 4th, Earth reckoning. Two months! A month for the journey to Earth and a month—for what?

As Mrs. Corliss slipped quietly into a dreamless sleep, Cross had the answer. He dared not waste another day searching for the true slans. Later, perhaps, that trail could be picked up again, but now, if he could get out of this—

He frowned mentally. Within minutes he would be under physical examination by members of the most ruthless, most thoroughgoing and efficient race in the solar system. In spite of his successful attempt at delay, in spite of his preliminary success in getting a crystal into the hands of one of his escort, luck had been against him. Ingraham was not curious enough to take the crystal out of his pocket and open it. He'd have to make another attempt, of course, but that was desperate. No slan would be anything but suspicious at such a second try, no matter how the approach was made.

His thought stopped. His mind stilled to a state of reception as an almost inaudible voice spoke from Ingraham's radic, and the words flowed across the surface of Ingraham's mind.

"Physical examination completed or not, you will bring Barton Corliss immediately before me. That supersedes any previous order."

"O.K., Joanna!" Ingraham replied quite audibly. He turned. "You're to be taken at once before Joanna Hillory, the military commissioner."

It was Prentice who echoed the thought in Cross' mind. The tall slan said, "Joanna is the only one of us who spent hours with Cross. She was appointed commissioner with that experience and her subsequent studies of him in mind. She supervised the world-wide successful search for his hide-out and she also predicted the failure of the attack that was made with cyclotron. In addition, she's written a lengthy report outlining in minutest detail the hours she spent in his company. If you're Cross, she'll recognize you in one minute flat."

Cross was silent. He had no way of evaluating the tall slan's statement, but he suspected that it might be true.

As Cross emerged from the case room, he had his first glimpse of the city of Cimmerium, the true, the underground city. From the doorway he could see along two corridors. One led back to the elevator down which he had come, the other to a broad expanse of tall, transparent doors. Beyond the doors lay a city of dreams.

It had been said on Earth that the secret of the materials that made up the walls of the grand palace had been lost. But here in this hidden city of the tendrilless slans was all the glory of it, and more. There was a street of soft, changing colours, and the magnificent realization of that age-old dream of architects, form-perfect buildings that were *alive* as music was alive. Here was—and no other word could apply, because no word in his knowledge was suitable—here was the gorgeous equivalent in architecture of the highest form of music.

Out in the street, he cut the beauty of it from his mind. Only the people mattered. And there were thousands in the buildings, in bustling cars and on foot. Thousands of minds within reach of a mind that missed nothing and searched now for one, just one, true slan.

And there was none; not a trace of betraying mind whisper; not a brain that did not *know* its owner was a trendrilless slan. Definitely, finally, the leaky brain shields gave of their knowledge. His conviction that they must be here was shattered, as his life would now be. Wherever the true slans were, their protection was slan-proof, beyond logic. But then, of course, logic had said that monster babies were not created by decent folk. The facts, it happened, were otherwise. What facts? Hearsay? But what other explanation was there?

"Here we are!" Ingraham said quietly.

Bradshaw said, "Come along, Corliss, Miss Hillory will see you now . . . alone!"

The floor felt strangely hard beneath his feet as he walked the hundred feet to the open door. Her inner sanctum was large and cosy, and it looked like a private den rather than a business office. There were books on shelves. Against one wall was a small electric filing cabinet. There was a soft-toned sofa and multi-pneumatic chairs and a deep-piled rug. And finally there was a great gleaming desk behind which sat a proud, smiling, youthful woman.

Cross had not expected Joanna Hillory to look older, and she didn't. Another fifty years might put lines into those velvet-smooth cheeks, but now there was only one difference, and that was in himself. Years before, a boy slan had gazed at this glorious woman; now his eyes held the cool appraisal of maturity.

He noted curiously that her gaze was eager-bright, and that seemed out of place. His mind concentrated. The co-ordinated power of his sense abruptly dissolved her facial expression into triumph and a genuine joy. Alertly, his brain pressed against her mind shield, probing at the tiny gaps, absorbing every leak of thought, analysing every overtone, and second by second his puzzlement grew. Her smile flashed into soft laughter; and then her shield went down. Her mind lay before him, exposed to his free, untrammeled gaze. Simultaneously, a thought formed in her brain:

"Look deep, John Thomas Cross, and know first that all Porgrave receivers in this room and vicinity have been disconnected. Know, too, that I am your only living friend, and that I ordered you brought before me to forestall a physical examination which you could not possibly survive. I watched you through the Porgraves and, finally, I knew it was you. But hurry, search my mind, verify my good will, and then we must act swiftly to save your life!"

There was no credulity, no trustfulness, in his brain. The moments fled, and still he probed the dark corridors of her brain searching for those basic reasons that alone could explain this wondrous thing. At last he said quietly:

"So you believed in the ideals of a fifteen-year-old, caught fire from a young egotist who offered only—"

"Hope!" she finished. "You brought hope just before I reached the point where most slans become as hard and ruthless as life can make them. 'Human beings,' you said, 'what about human beings?' And the shock of that and other things affected me beyond recovery. I deliberately gave a false description of you. You may have wondered about that. I passed it off because I was not supposed to have an expert's knowledge of human physiology. I didn't, of course, but I could have drawn you from memory perfectly, and the picture grew clearer every day. It was considered natural that I become a student of the Cross affair. And natural, also, that I was appointed to most of the supervisory positions that had any connection with you. I suppose that it was equally natural that—"

She stopped almost expectantly, and Cross said gravely, "I'm sorry about that!"

Her grey eyes met his brown ones steadily. "Whom else will you marry?" she asked. "A normal life must include marriage. Of course, I know nothing of your relationship to the slan girl, Kathleen Layton, except that you were with her at her death. But marriage to several women, frequently at the same time, is not unusual in slan history. Then, of course, there is my age."

"I recognize," Cross said simply, "that fifteen or twenty years is not the slightest obstacle to marriage among long-lived slans. It happens, however, that I have a mission."

"Whether as wife or not," said Joanna Hillory, "from this hour you have a companion on that mission provided we can get you through this physical examination alive."

"Oh, that!" Cross waved a hand. "All I needed was time and a method of getting certain crystals into the hands of Ingraham and the others. You have provided both. We'll also need the paralyser gun in the drawer of your desk. And then call them in one at a time."

With one sweeping movement of her hand, she drew the gun from the drawer. "I'll do the shooting!" she said. "Now what?"

Cross laughed softly at Joanna Hillory's vehemence and felt a strange wonder at the turn of events, even now that he was sure. For years he had lived on nerve and cold determination. Abruptly, something of her fire touched him. His eyes gleamed.

"And you won't regret what you have done, though your faith may be tried to the utmost before we are finished. This attack on Earth must not take place. Not now, not until we know what to do with those poor devils aside from holding them down by force. Tell me, is there any way I can get to Earth? I read in Corliss' mind something about a plan to transfer to Earth all slans resembling me. Can that be done?"

"It can. The decision rests entirely with me."

"Then," said Cross grimly, "the time has come for quick action. I must get to Earth. I must go to the palace. I must see Kier Gray."

The perfect mouth parted in a smile, but there was no humour in her fine eyes. "And how," she asked softly, "are you going to get near the palace, with its fortifications?"

"My mother spoke often of the secret passages under the palace," Cross answered. "Perhaps your statistics machine will know the exact location of the various entrances."

"The machine!" said Joanna Hillory, and was momentarily silent. Finally: "Yes, the 'Stics knows. It knows many things. Come along."

In the outer room, he followed her as she led the way in and out among row on row of great, thick, shiny, metallic plates. This, Cross knew, was the Bureau of Statistics, and these plates were the electric filing cabinets that yielded their information at the touch of a button, the spelling out of a name, a number, a key word. No one knew (so Corliss' mind had informed him) how much information was in those cabinets. They had been brought from Earth, and dated back to the earliest slan days. A quadrillion facts were there for the asking. Included, no doubt, was the entire story of the seven-year search for one John Thomas Cross

—the search that Joanna Hillory had directed from the inner sanctum of this very building.

Joanna Hillory said, "I want to show you something."

He stood watching her as she pushed the name plates "Samuel Lann" and then "Natural Mutation." Swiftly, then, her fingers touched the activating button, and read on the glowing plate:

"Excerpts from Samuel Lann's diary, June 1, 2071: Today, I had another look at the three babies, and there is no doubt that here is an extraordinary mutation. I have seen human beings with tails. I have examined cretins and idiots, and the monsters that have turned up in such numbers recently. And I have observed those curious, dreadful, organic developments that human beings are subject to. But this is the opposite of such horrors. This is perfection.

"Two girls and a boy. What a grand and tremendous accident. If I were not a cold-blooded rationalist, the exact rightness of what has happened would make me a blubbering worshipper at the shrine of metaphysics. Two girls to reproduce their kind, and one boy to mate with them. I'll have to train them to the idea.

"June 2, 2071," began the machine. But Joanna pressed urgently at the dissolver, manipulated the number key, and produced "June 7, 2073":

"A damn fool journalist wrote an article about the children today. The ignoramus stated that I had used a machine on their mother, whereas I didn't even know the woman till after the children were born. I'll have to persuade the parents to retreat to some remote part of the world. Anything could happen where there are human beings—superstitious, emotional asses."

Joanna Hillory made another selection—"May 31, 2088":

"Their seventeenth birthday. The girls thoroughly accept the idea of mating with their brother. Morality, after all, is a matter of training. I want this mating to take place, even though I found those other youngsters last year. I think it unwise to wait till these latter grow up. We can start crossbreeding later."

It was August 18, 2090, that produced: "Each of the girls had triplets. Wonderful. At this rate of reproduction, the period when chance can destroy them will soon be reduced to an actuarial minimum. Despite the fact that others of their kind are turning up here and there, I am continually impressing on the children that their descendants will be the future rulers of the world. . . ."

Back in her office, Joanna Hillory faced him and said, "You see, there is not, there never has been, a slan-making machine. All slans are natural mutations."

She broke off abruptly: "The best entrance to the palace for your purpose is located in the statuary section, two miles inside the grounds, constantly under brilliant lights, and directly under the guns of the first line of heavy fortifications. Also, machine-gun emplacements and tank patrols control the first two miles."

"What about my gun? Would I be allowed to have it on Earth?"

"No. The plan of transferring the men resembling you includes their disarmament."

He was aware of her questioning gaze on him, and his lean face twisted into a frown.

"What kind of man is Kier Gray, according to your records?"

"Enormously capable, for a human being. Our secret X-rays definitely show him as human, if that's what you're thinking."

"At that time I did think about that, but your words verify Kathleen Layton's experience."

"We've got off the track," Joanna Hillory said. "What about the fortifications?"

He shook his head, smiling humourlessly. "When the stakes are great, risks must match them. Naturally, I shall go alone. You"—he gazed at her sombrely—"will have the great trust of locating the cave where my ship is, and getting the machine through to Earth before June 10th. Corliss, also, will have to be released. And now, please call Ingraham in."

18

THE RIVER seemed wider than when Cross had last seen it. Uneasily, he stared across the quarter mile of swirling waters. In the swift current were patches of darkness and light, reflections from the ever-changing wonder-fire of the palace. There was late spring snow in the concealing brush where he removed his clothing, and it tingled coldly against his bare feet when he stood at last stripped for his task.

He held his mind almost blank. Then came the ironic realization that one naked man against the world was a sorry symbol of the atomic energy he controlled. He'd had so many weapons and not used them when he could. And now this ring on his finger, with its tiny atomic generator, and its pitiful two-foot effective range—this was the only product of his years of effort that he dared to take with him into the fortress.

Trees on the opposite bank made shadows half across the river. The darkness streaked the ugly swell of racing water, which carried him half a mile downstream before his long backstrokes finally brought him to the shelter of the shallows.

He lay there, his mind reconnoitering the thoughts that came from the two machine-gunners hidden in the trees. Cautiously, he edged into a patch of concealing brush and donned his clothes. He lay then, patient as an old tiger stalking its prey. There was a clearing to be crossed, and it was too far for hypnotic control. The moment of their carelessness came abruptly. He covered the fifty yards in a fraction over three seconds.

One man never knew what struck him. The other jerked around, his long thin face strained and ghastly in the flicker of light that peered through the foliage. But there was no stopping, no evading the blow that caught his jaw and smashed him to the ground. In fifteen minutes of crystalless hypnotism, they were under control. Fifteen minutes! Eight an hour! He smiled ironically. That certainly precluded any possibility of hypnotically overpowering the palace with its ten thousand or so men. He must have key men.

He brought the two prisoners back to consciousness and gave them his orders. Silently they took their portable machine guns and fell in behind him. They knew every inch of the ground. They knew when the tank patrols rolled by on their night rounds. There were no better soldiers in the human army than these palace guards. In two hours there were a dozen trained fighters slipping along like shadows, working in a silent, swift co-ordination that needed only an occasional soft-spoken command.

In three more hours, he had altogether seventeen men, a colonel, a captain and three lieutenants. And ahead was the long cordon of exquisite statuary, sparkling fountains and blazing lights that marked at once his goal and the end of the first simple operation.

The first hint of the coming dawn misted the eastern sky as Cross lay with his little army in the shadows of shrubbery and stared across the quarter mile of brilliantly lighted area. He could see the dark line of woods on the other side, where the fortifications were hidden.

"Unfortunately," the colonel whispered, "there is no chance of tricking them. The jurisdiction of this unit ends right here. It is forbidden to cross to any one of the dozen fortified rings without a pass, and even a pass can be used only in the daytime."

Cross frowned. There were precautions here beyond his expectations, and he saw that their strictness was of recent enactment. The slan attack on his valley, though no one believed the wild peasant tales about the size of the ships involved or suspected they were spaceships, had produced tension and alertness that might defeat him now.

"Captain!"

"Yes?" The tall officer slid up beside him.

"Captain, you look the most like me. You will, therefore, exchange your uniform for my clothes and then you, all of you, will return to your regular stations."

He watched them slip off and vanish into the darkness. Then he stood up with the stiff carriage of the captain, and stalked into the light. Ten feet, twenty, thirty... He could see the fountain he wanted, a glittering shape with its sparkling streams of water. But there was too much artificial light, there were too many minds around, a confusion of vibrations that must be interfering with the one thought wave his mind was reaching for, if the damned thing was still there after all these hundreds of years. If it weren't there, God help him!

Forty feet, fifty, sixty . . . and then to his tense brain came a whisper, the tiniest of tiny mind vibrations.

"*To any slan who penetrates this far—there is a secret passage into the palace. The five-flower design on the white fountain due north is a combination knob that operates on a secret door by radio. The combination is . . .*"

He had known—the 'Stics machine had known—that the secret was in the fountain, but no more than that. Now—

A harsh magnified voice smashed out from the far trees: "Who the devil are you? What do you want? Get back to your

146

commanding officer, obtain a pass and return in the morning. Quick!"

He was at the fountain, his swift fingers on the flower design, his body and action half hidden from the host of staring, suspicious eyes. And there was not an ounce of energy to spare from his intense concentration. Before that singleness of purpose, the combination yielded, and a second thought came from a second Porgrave broadcaster:

"The door is now open. It is an extremely narrow tunnel leading down through dense darkness. The mouth is in the centre of the equestrian group of statuary a hundred feet due north. Have courage. . . ."

It was not courage that was lacking. It was time. A hundred feet north, toward the palace, *toward* those menacing forts. Cross laughed curtly. The ancient builder of the secret entrance had certainly picked a hell of a spot to practise his ingenuity. He walked on, even as the harsh voice lashed out again.

"You out there . . . you will stop at once, or we fire. Return to your district, and consider yourself under arrest. At once!"

"I've got a very important message!" Cross called out in a clear voice that was as similar to the captain's as he could make it without practice. "Emergency!"

And still they didn't consider one man dangerous. Still he walked on. The answer blared back:

"No possible emergency justifies such a flagrant breach of regulations. Return immediately to your district . . . I warn you for the last time!"

He stared down at the little black hole, and dismay struck into him, a piercing claustrophobia, the first he had ever known, black and terrible as the tunnel itself. Entrust himself to the rabbit's burrow with its potentialities of suffocation, possibly to be buried alive in some cunningly contrived human trap! There could be no certainty that they had not discovered this, as they had already discovered so many other slan hideaways.

Abruptly it was urgent. A torrent of sibilant pulsations reached out of the trees ahead, little whispers that breathed against his brain like soft physical things. Somebody saying, "Sergeant, train your gun on him!"

"What about the horse statuary, sir? Be a shame to nick them!"

"Aim at his legs and then at his head!"

And that was that. With clenched teeth, body stiff and straight, and arms flung over his head, he leaped like a diver going feet first, and came down so perfectly in the tunnel that it was several seconds before his clothes scraped the vertical walls.

The passage was smooth as glass, and it was only after Cross had fallen an immense distance that it started to tilt away from the vertical. Pressure of friction grew stronger; and after more swift seconds, he was sliding at a distinct angle that grew flatter by the instant. His breathless speed slowed measurably. He saw a glimmer of light ahead. Abruptly he emerged into a low-roofed, dimly lighted corridor. His line of motion was still slightly downward, but it straightened rapidly. His journey ended, he lay dizzily on his back, his vision spinning.

A dozen revolving lights above him gradually tightened their circle and became a single, dim bulb shedding a dull refulgence around it: a wan, almost futile, light, that hugged the ceiling and melted into darkness before it reached the floor. Cross climbed to his feet, and found himself staring at a sign that was just high enough up on the wall for the ceiling light to touch it. He strained and read.

"You are now two miles below the surface. The tunnel behind you is blocked by steel and concrete shafts, which were actuated, each in its turn, by your passage. It will take an hour to get from here to the palace. Slans are forbidden under severe penalties to enter the palace proper. Take heed."

There was a tickling in his throat. He fought back the sneeze but it came, followed by a half dozen more. The tears ran down his cheeks. It was dimmer where he stood than when he had first come into the corridor. The long row of ceiling lights, which faded into the remote distance ahead, were not as bright as they had been. Dust obscured them.

Cross bent in the half darkness and ran his fingers lightly over the floor. A soft, thick carpet of dust lay there. He peered ahead, searching for footprints that would show that this corridor had been recently used. But there was only the dust, an inch at least, years of it.

Countless years had passed since that order with its vague threat had been placed there. Meanwhile, there was more real danger. Human beings would now know where to look for the secret entrance. Before they discovered it, he must, in defiance of the slan law, penetrate the palace and get at Kier Gray!

It was a world of shadows and silence, and insidious choking fingers of dust that kept reaching for Cross' throat, and then—ludicrous paradox—tickled instead of strangled. He went through many doors and corridors, and great stately rooms.

Suddenly, there was a soft metal click behind him. Whirling, he saw a solid sheet of metal door flow softly into the floor over which he had just passed, creating a smooth, hard wall. He stood very still, and for a moment he was a sensitive machine receiving impressions. There was the long narrow corridor, ending just ahead, the dim lights above, and the floor beneath him, the latter cushioned by a thick, yielding dust. Into the silence a second click projected harshly. The walls creaked metallically and began to move, coming at a deliberate pace toward him, and toward each other.

Automatic, he decided, for there was not the faintest tendril of thought anywhere. Coolly, he examined the potentialities of the trap, and presently discovered at the extreme end of each wall a nook. Each nook was six feet four inches in height. A shallow place large enough to hold half a human body sideways. The contours of the body were grooved into those nooks.

Cross smiled grimly. In a few minutes, the walls would come together, and the only available space for him would be where the two nooks would then be joined. A neat trap!

True, the atomic energy of the ring on his finger could probably disintegrate a pathway for him through the walls or the door, but his purpose demanded that this trap be successful up to a point. He examined the nooks more carefully. This time his ring flashed twice in brief fury, dissolving the handcuffs that waited in the handholds for the helpless, carving also enough space to give himself freedom of movement.

When the walls were a foot apart, a four-inch-wide crack opened the full length of the floor, and the small mountain of dust poured into it. A few minutes later the two walls met with a metallic bang.

A moment of silence! Then machinery whirred faintly, and there was a swift flow of upward movement. The movement continued for minutes on end before it slowed and finally stopped. But the machinery still whispered beneath him. Another minute, and then the cubicle in which he stood began to revolve slowly. A crack appeared before his face, a crack that widened into a rectangular hole through which he could see into a room.

The machinery stopped whirring. There was silence again while Cross examined the room. There was a desk in the centre of a highly polished floor, with walnut-panelled walls beyond. Some chairs and filing cabinets and the edge of a floor-to-ceiling bookcase completed what he could see of the spare, businesslike room.

Footsteps sounded. The man who came in and shut the door behind him was magnificently built, greyed at the temples now, lines of age showing. But there was no one in all the world who would not have recognized that lean face, those piercing eyes, the ruthlessness that was written indelibly in those thin nostrils and line of jaw. It was a face too hard, too determined to be pleasant. But withal it was a noble countenance. Here was a born leader of men. Cross felt himself dissected, his face explored by those keen eyes. Finally, the proud mouth twisted into the faintest sneer.

Kier Gray said, "So you got caught. That wasn't very clever." It was the words that did it. For with them came surface thoughts, and those surface thoughts were a deliberate screen held over a mind shield as tight as his own. No leaky tendrilless slan shield this, but an enormous fact. Kier Gray, leader of men, was a man who believed himself to be—

"*A true slan!*"

That one explosive sentence Cross uttered, and then the fluidity of his mind chilled into an ice of quiet thought. All those years that Kathleen Layton had lived with Kier Gray, and not suspected the truth. Of course she had lacked experience with mind shields, and there had been John Petty with a similar type of shield to confuse the issue, because John Petty *was* human. How cleverly the dictator had imitated the human way of thought protection! Cross shook himself mentally and, determined to get reaction this time, repeated:

"So—you *are* a slan!"

The other's face twisted sardonically. "That's hardly the right description for a man without tendrils who cannot read minds, but yes, I am a slan."

He paused, then continued earnestly: "For hundreds of years we who knew the truth have existed for the purpose of preventing the tendrilless slans from taking over the world of men. What more natural than that we should insinuate our way into control of the human government? Are we not the most intelligent beings on the face of the Earth?"

Cross nodded. It fitted, of course. His own deductions had told him that. Once he knew that the true slans were not, actually, the hidden government of the tendrilless slans, it was inevitable they would be governing the human world, for all Kathleen's belief and the tendrilless slan X-ray pictures showing Kier Gray to be possessed of a human heart and other nonslan organs. Somewhere here there was still a tremendous mystery. He shook his head finally.

"I still don't get it all. I expected to find the true slans ruling the tendrilless . . . secretly. Everything fits, of course, in a distorted fashion. But why antislan propaganda? What about that slan ship which came to the palace years ago? Why are true slans hunted and killed like rats? Why not an arrangement with the tendrilless slans?"

The leader stared at him thoughtfully. "We have tried on occasion to tamper with antislan propaganda, one such attempt being that very ship to which you have referred. For special reasons I was forced to order it down in the marshes. But in spite of that apparent failure, it succeeded in its main purpose, which was to convince the tendrilless slans, who were definitely contemplating their attack, that we were still a force to be reckoned with.

"It was the palpable weakness of the silver ship that convinced the tendrilless slans. They knew we could not be that impotent and so once more they hesitated and were lost. It has always been unfortunate, the number of true slans being killed in various parts of the world. They are the descendants of slans who, scattered after the War of Disaster, never made connection with the slan organization. After the tendrilless slans came on the scene it was, of course, too late to do anything. Our enemies were in a position to interfere with every communication device that we possessed.

"We tried our best, naturally, to contact such wanderers. But the only ones who really got through were those who came to the palace to kill me. For them we provided a number of easy passageways into the palace. My instruments tell me that you came the hard way, through one of the ancient entrances. Very daring. We can use another bold young man in our small organization."

Cross stared at the other coolly. Kier Gray obviously did not suspect his identity nor did he know how near was the hour of tendrilless slan attack. It made the moment a great one as he said: "I'm amazed that you allowed me to catch you by surprise like this."

Kier Gray's smile faded abruptly. He said in a tight voice:

"Your remark is very pointed. You assume that you have caught me. Either you are a fool, a possibility refuted by your obvious intelligence, or else, in spite of your apparent imprisonment, that imprisonment is not actual. And there's only one man in the world who could nullify the hard steel of the handcuffs in that cubicle."

Amazingly, the strong face had gone slack, the hard lines were faded, but it was the eyes that showed strength now. A glad, eager, wide-eyed joy. He half whispered:

"Man, man, *you've done it*! in spite of my being unable to give you the slightest help . . . atomic energy in its great form at last."

His voice rang out then, clear and triumphant:

"John Thomas Cross, I welcome you and your father's discovery. Come in here and sit down. Wait a minute while I get you out of that damn place! We can talk here in this private den of mine. No human being is ever allowed here."

The wonder of it grew with each passing minute. The tremendousness of what it meant, this world-wide balancing of immense forces. True slans with the human beings, who knew not of their masters, against the tendrilless slans who, in spite of their brilliant, far-flung organization, had never guessed the truth behind the mystery.

"Naturally," said Kier Gray, "your discovery that slans are naturals and not machine-made is nothing new to us. We are the mutation-after-man. The forces of that mutation were at work many years before that great day when Samuel Lann realized the pattern of perfection in some of the mutations. It is only too obvious now in retrospect that nature was building for a tremendous attempt. Cretins increased alarmingly; insanity advanced by enormous percentages. The amazing thing about it was the speed with which the web of biological forces struck everywhere across the Earth.

"We have always assumed far too readily that no cohesion exists between individuals, that the race of men is not a unit with an immensely tenuous equivalent of a blood-and-nerve stream flowing from man to man. There are, of course, other ways of explaining why billions of people can be made to act alike, think alike, feel alike, given a single dominating stimulus, but slan philosophers have, through the ages, been toying with the possibility that such mental affinity is the product of an extraordinary unity, physical as well as mental.

"For hundreds, perhaps thousands, of years, the tensions had been building up. And then in a single stupendous quarter of a millennium more than a billion abnormal births occurred. It was like a cataclysm that paralysed the human will. The truth was lost in a wave of terror that swept the world into war. All attempts to revive the truth have been swamped by an incredible mass hysteria . . . even now, after a thousand years. Yes, I said a *thousand* years. Only we true slans know that the nameless period actually lasted five hundred hellish years. And that the slan children discovered by Samuel Lann were born nearly fifteen hundred years ago.

"So far as we know, very few of those ultra-normal births were alike. Most were horrible failures, and there was only an occasional perfection. Even these would have been lost if Lann had failed to recognize them for what they were. Nature relied on the law of averages. No preconceived plan existed. What happened seemed simply to have been a reaction to the countless intolerable pressures that were driving men mad, because neither their minds nor their bodies were capable of withstanding modern civilization. These pressures being more or less similar, it is understandable that many of nature's botches should bear a resemblance to each other, without being similar in detail.

"An example of the enormous strength of that biological tide, and also of the fundamental unity of man," Kier Gray continued, "is shown in that nearly all slans born in the first few hundred years were triplets or, at lowest, twins. There are few such multiple births now. The single child is the rule. The wave has spent itself. Nature's part of the work ended, it remained for intelligence to carry on. And that was where the difficulty came.

"During the nameless period, slans were hunted like wild beasts. There is no modern parallel for the ferocity of human beings against the people they considered responsible for the disaster. It was impossible to organize effectively. Our fore-fathers tried everything: underground hide-outs, surgical removal of tendrils, replacement of human hearts for their own double hearts, use of skinlike stuff over tendrils. But it proved useless.

"Suspicion was swift beyond all resistance. Men denounced their neighbours, and had them medically examined. The police made their raids on the vaguest of clues. The greatest difficulty of all was the birth of babies. Even where a successful disguise had been achieved by the parents, the arrival of a child was always a period of immense danger, and all too frequently brought death to mother, father and child. It was gradually realized that the race could not survive. The scattered remnants of the slans finally concentrated on efforts to control the mutation force. At last they found how to shape the large molecules that made up the genes themselves. It proved to be the ultimate life stuff that controlled the genes as the genes in their turn controlled the shape of the organs and the body.

"It remained then to experiment. That took two hundred precarious years. No risks could be taken with the race, though individuals risked their lives and their health. They found at last how complex groups of molecules could control the form of each organ for one generation or many. Alter the pattern of that group, and the organ affected was transformed, only to turn up again in a later generation. And so they changed the basic slan structure, keeping what was good and had survival value, eliminating what had proved dangerous. The genes controlling the tendrils were altered, transferring the mind-reading ability inside the brain, but insuring that that ability did not turn up for many generations—"

Cross interrupted with a gasp: "Wait a minute! When I first started to search for the true slans, logic said they were infiltrated into the tendrilless slan organization. Are you trying to tell me that the tendrilless slans will eventually *be* the true slans?"

Kier Gray nodded matter-of-factly. "In less than fifty years they'll have the ability to read minds, although the faculty will for a time be located inside their minds. Eventually, of course, the tendrils will come back. We haven't discovered yet whether we can make any change permanent."

Cross said, "But why were they ever stopped from having the mind-reading ability—particularly during these decisive years?"

The reply was earnestly spoken: "I can see that you still do not recognize the inescapable realities of the lives of our ancestors. The capacity and knowledge of mind reading were withheld because it was necessary to observe psychological reactions . . .

because as people acted not knowing they were true slans, so they would have acted knowing it. What happened?

"We—the slan leaders—had altered so many of their distinguishing organs to protect them from predatory human beings that they acted as if they had no interest in being anything but quiet-living folk in the remote corners of the world. The truth might have roused them, but not in time. We have discovered that slans are by nature antiwar, antimurder, antiviolence. We used every argument, but no logic would produce anything more than the general feeling that in a hundred years or so they would start thinking in terms of action.

"It was impossible to permit them to stay that way. Human existence has been like a bomb fuse. Life burned slowly for millions of years, then the fire reached the bomb—which exploded. The explosion managed to set another fuse alight, but, though we only suspected it then, the old bomb and fuse were finished. Now, it is certain that human beings will sputter out, vanish from the Earth as a result of the sterility that has already started on a vast scale, though it is not yet noticeable. Man will go into history along with the Java ape man, the Neanderthal beast man, and the Cro-Magnon primitive. Undoubtedly, the sterility which will cause this will be blamed on the slans, and when human beings discover it there will begin the second great wave of ferocity and terrorism. Nothing but the most powerful organization, expanded at top acceleration, under constant and dangerous pressure, could have been properly prepared."

"And so," Cross said softly, "you drove out the tendrilless . . . the protected . . . slans with violence that bewildered them, then brought an equally ruthless reaction. Ever since you've been a spur on their expansion and a check on that artificially engendered, ruthless spirit of theirs. But why haven't you told them the truth?"

The leader smiled grimly. "We tried that, but those we selected as confidants thought it was a trick, and their logic led them instantly to our hiding place. We had to murder them all. We've got to wait till the mind-reading ability comes back.

"And now, from what you've told me, I can see that we must act swiftly. Your hypnotism crystals, of course, could be the final solution to the problem of human antagonism. As soon as there are enough slans with the know-how, that difficulty at least may be overcome. As for the imminent attack—"

He reached toward a buzzer button on his desk, and pressed it.

He went on, "That will bring a few colleagues of mine. We must have an immediate conference."

Cross said slowly, "Slans can safely hold conferences in the grand palace?"

Kier Gray smiled. "My friend, we base our operations upon the limitations of individual human beings."

"I'm not sure I understand."

"It's quite simple. Years ago, many human beings knew a lot about many of the secret passageways of the palace. One of my first acts, as soon as I was able, was to classify this knowledge. Then, one by one, I transferred to other parts of the world the men who had the information. There, isolated in various obscure government departments, they were skilfully assassinated."

He shook his head grimly. "It doesn't take long. And, once the secret has been established, the very vastness of this place—and the strict military control of every avenue—prevents rediscovery. There are seldom less than a hundred slans around the palace. Most of them are tendrilled, although a few tendrilless ones—descendants, like myself, of the earliest successful volunteers for the survival experiments in gene transformation—have always known the truth and been part of our organization. We could operate on the tendrilled ones, of course, and make it safe for them to go outside, but we've reached the stage where we want a few tendrilled slans around, so that the others can see what their descendants will be like in a few generations. After all, we don't want *them* suddenly becoming panicky."

"What about Kathleen?" asked Cross slowly.

The older man gave him a long, measured look, and said finally, "Kathleen was an experiment. I wanted to see if human beings who grew up with a slan might not come to realize that kinship was possible. When it was finally evident that this could not be achieved, I decided to transfer her here, to these secret chambers, where she could begin to benefit from association with other slans, and help in all the things that had to be done. She proved to be bolder and more ingenious than I had anticipated—but you know about that escapade."

The word "escapade" was about as mild a description of a major tragedy as Cross had ever heard. Evidently, this man was even more inured to death than he was. Before he could comment, Kier Gray said:

"My own wife, who was a true slan, fell victim to the secret police in a somewhat different, though equally grim, manner, except that in her case I was not present until long after—" He stopped. For a long moment he sat with narrowed eyes, and there was nothing casual about his manner now. He said abruptly, "And now that I've told you so much—what *is* your father's secret?"

Cross said simply, "I can go into it in greater detail later. Briefly, my father rejected the notion of critical mass, on which the first bombs were based. Atomic energy is available that way—in torrents, in explosive form, in the form of heat, and for certain medical and industrial purposes. But it is almost impossible to control for direct use. My father rejected it partly because it was useless to slans in that form, partly because he had a theory.

"He also rejected the massive cyclotron principle, but it was the cyclotron that gave him at least a part of his great idea. He evolved a central core of positive electrons spun out like a fine wire. At this core, but not directly at it—a comparison would be the way a comet comes at the Sun in an elongated orbit—at this 'Sun' he discharged his negative-electron 'comets' at the speed of light.

"The 'Sun' whipped the comets around and flung them out into 'space,' where—and here the comparison is very real—a second positive core which might be called 'Jupiter' pulls at the 'comets' already travelling at the speed of light, and catapults them *faster than light* completely out of their orbits. At that speed, each electron becomes matter in a minus state, with a destructive power utterly out of proportion to its 'size'. Normal matter loses its coherence in the presence of this minus stuff and reverts instantly to a primeval state. It—"

He paused, and looked up as the door opened. Three men with golden slan tendrils in their hair came in. Their mind shields went down as they saw him; Cross lowered his a moment later. There was a lightning interchange among the four of them: names, back history, purposes—data of every kind necessary to a fuller comprehension of the meeting. The process was dazzling to Cross, who, except for his brief contact with the inexperienced Kathleen, and his undeveloped childhood relationship with his parents, had previously only imagined how effective such an interchange might be.

He was so intent that he was caught by surprise when the door opened again.

A tall young woman came in. She had flashing eyes, and a strong, mature, finely moulded, delicately textured face. Looking at her, his muscles stiffened, his nerves grew taut and a chill enveloped his body. Yet, even as his amazement grew, he thought with a sharp logic that he should have realized after the way the smashed head of Mrs. Corliss had been repaired on far-off Mars. He should have known the moment he discovered that Kier Gray was a true slan. Should have guessed, knowing the hates and envies of the palace, that only death, and a return from death in secret, could ultimately and effectively keep Kathleen safe from John Petty.

It was at that point in his thought that Kier Gray's voice cut across the silence with the rich tones of one who had secretly relished this instant for years:

"Jommy Cross, I want you to meet Kathleen Layton Gray . . . my daughter."

156

Other Panthers For Your Enjoyment

Isaac Asimov, Grand Master of Science Fiction, in Panther Books

More Great Science Fiction Books from Panther

Panther Science Fiction — A Selection from the World's Best S.F. List

All these books are available at your local bookshop or newsagent; or can be ordered direct from the publisher. Just tick the titles you want and fill in the form below.

Name..

Address..

....

Write to Panther Cash Sales, PO Box 11, Falmouth, Cornwall TR10 9EN
Please enclose remittance to the value of the cover price plus 15p postage and packing for one book plus 5p for each additional copy. Overseas customers please send 20p for first book and 10p for each additional book.
Granada Publishing reserve the right to show new retail prices on covers, which may differ from those previously advertised in the text or elsewhere.